# HERA

# SPEED DATING WITH THE DENIZENS OF THE UNDERWORLD

# BOOK TWENTY

## GINA KINCADE

NAUGHTY NIGHTS PRESS LLC • CANADA

HERA

SPEED DATING WITH THE DENIZENS OF
THE UNDERWORLD
BOOK TWENTY

COPYRIGHT © 2022

GINA KINCADE

ISBN: 978-1-77357-444-8

978-1-77357-445-5

PUBLISHED BY NAUGHTY NIGHTS PRESS LLC

COVER ART BY KING COVER DESIGNS

# HERA

**It's all work and no play until the denizens of the underworld have had enough of the rain.**

Goddess Hera Aarden lives in the underworld, enjoying her new life as the co-owner of the ButterNut Bakery. With her small side business of hand brewed potions, creams, and tinctures literally flying off the shelves, business is booming, which means Hera is too busy for much of a social life. But she's lonely and the one-night stands she used to go for just aren't scratching that annoying itch anymore.

The denizens of the underworld are fed up with the rainy season, so it's time to shake things up, and the Goddess of Love and her toothy sidekick have just the thing to put the pep back in Hera's step.

# HERA

There should be nothing but clear skies and sunshine ahead now!

Augustine McKellen and his two brothers have been dreaming of their fated mates, yet none are brave enough to do anything about it until August gives in and ventures out, eventually stumbling across the new speed dating at the DeLux Cafe. Even if the term "speed dating" implies something fast and furious, which isn't really what he's after, August has to get his old school dragon booty out there or he will never find his mate.

Once he's met the perfect woman for him, will she be able to accept his beastly side, scales and all?

*Hera is book twenty in the Speed Dating with the Denizens of the Underworld shared world series, filled with bold and beautiful goddesses, dashing gentleman dragon shifters, and more.*

# CHAPTER ONE

"HERA!" DEMI SHOUTED from the other end of the apartment the sisters shared.

Hera sighed and swirled the potion she was in the middle of completing. She made a notation in her lab book so she could come back to it and left the room that Demi called her chemistry lab. She glided through the main living space of their apartment, the rugs soft on her bare feet and protecting her from the beautifully polished hardwood underneath. She found Demi on her knees in her bedroom, her head in the depths of her closet. "What is it, sister dear?" Hera asked.

Demi gave a little squeak of surprise and sat back on her heels, her long, dark hair in complete disarray. "Have you seen my white heels?"

"Why are you searching for them the mundane way?" Hera asked, puzzled. She pulled at the air and a pair of white high heels appeared in her hands. "Is this a 'playing at being human' thing?"

Demi blushed and got to her feet. "No, I'm just so flustered that I forgot about that."

Hera smirked. "Charles is looking forward to you moving in as well. You know that anything you forget, you can pick up after work one day. I'm not going to ban you from the apartment."

"You're right," Demi said with a chuckle. Her suitcase closed with a thought, the zipper flying around the edge. "Are you going to be all right here, all by yourself?"

"Of course, I will be." Hera brushed off her sister's concern. "And if I'm lonely, I can always—"

"Hook up with a random supe?" Demi finished for her.

"I was *going to say* get a roommate," Hera declared huffily, crossing her arms under her ample bosom.

"Right, " Demi said skeptically.

Hera relented and hugged her sister. "Maybe I'll come visit you topside."

Demi gasped happily and held Hera at arms length. "Would you really? We would love to have you. The lake house is beautiful."

"Once you've settled in a bit," Hera said, taken aback by how thrilled her sister seemed to be by the flippant suggestion. Hera hadn't been topside in… Well, since she had moved to Purgatory to live with her sister. She suppressed a shudder. She was very happy living here, more so since Lucifer, the ruler of Purgatory, had cleaned up the place a bit for his love, Chloe.

The doorbell rang.

"I'll get that. You keep packing," Hera said, giving Demi a light kiss on the cheek. "Charles is expecting you soon, isn't he?"

"Yes, he is!" Suddenly, the room had four more packed suitcases and Demi's hair was controlled in a long flowing braid. "Too much?"

Hera laughed. "Perfect."

The sisters walked to the door together, the suitcases trailing behind like ducklings following their mother.

"Chloe!" Hera said as she opened the door. "How unexpected! Please, come in."

"I don't mean to interrupt..." Chloe said, looking at the luggage. "Are you going on a trip?"

"Moving in with Charles," Demi said. "For a month. We're calling it a trial run." Her face crumpled. "What if it doesn't work out?" she gasped, her voice suddenly thick with tears.

"Nonsense!" Chloe said. "You'll be fine. Learn to compromise on the things that aren't important, and communicate when things are."

"Yes, I can do that." As if the sudden

panic had never happened, Demi was all smiles again.

Hera hugged her once more. "My blessing upon you," she whispered in Demi's ear, and then Demi vanished with her bags. Hera turned to her guest. "Please, come and sit. Can I get you anything?"

Chloe sat on one of the finely carved chairs overflowing with pillows. She put a hand over her lower belly and gave Hera puppy dog eyes. "Some lemonade would be amazing. And... Would you happen to have any raw carrots? I just got a wild craving for them."

"You got it," Hera said with a chuckle, heading for the kitchen.

"And ground cinnamon!" Chloe's voice echoed from the living space.

Hera returned with a pitcher of

lemonade, a plate of carrot sticks, and a bowl of cinnamon.

"You are a lifesaver!" Chloe declared dramatically, taking a carrot stick and dipping it in the cinnamon. She took a big bite and moaned. "Delicious."

Hiding her amusement behind her glass of lemonade, Hera watched her guest demolish another two carrot sticks in the same fashion before she apparently felt sated enough to put the plate down.

"Thank you so much," Chloe said cheerfully. "I'm really glad you were home today. I wanted to talk to you, professionally, if you don't mind."

"Professionally as the ButterNut Bakery's accountant, or...?" Hera let the question hang between the two women.

"Perhaps, as both. When we have the

baby shower, will you provide the cupcakes?"

"Of course. We would be delighted." Hera couldn't resist teasing a bit. "We'll make carrot cupcakes with cinnamon icing."

Chloe chuckled. "My cravings will be drastically different by then. Don't even get me started." She rolled her eyes. "One day last week, all I wanted for dinner was lettuce. Nothing else would do."

"Sounds like you're thirsty. Keep drinking your fluids," Hera advised.

"Oh, I am." Chloe poured herself a glass of lemonade. "But sometimes that isn't what I want."

Hera nodded sympathetically.

Chloe fluttered her hand not holding the glass. "You've distracted me! I didn't come here to talk about that. I need your help with a potion.”

“What kind of potion?” Hera asked, curious.

“We had an ultrasound today.” Chloe traced the condensation on the glass.

When she didn't say anything further, Hera prodded gently, “Is everything all right with the baby?”

“Oh! Yes, everything's fine.” Chloe smiled. “She's doing just fine.”

“A girl!” Hera clasped her hands.

“Yes. She's a bit larger than expected at twenty weeks, though.” Chloe bit her lip. “I'm worried it will be a difficult birth. Hera, will you promise me that you'll come when I call for you? Will you please attend her birth?”

“Of course I will, dear.” Hera took Chloe's hand in hers. “I will give you a potion in a few months—fresh is best—for you to take when you feel contractions. Real ones, mind, not Braxton-Hicks. The best time to take it... Oh, never mind me telling you, now, there's no way you'll remember. I'll write it all down and give it to you with the potion."

"That is such a relief!" Chloe relaxed back into the cushioned back of the chair. "I've been all over the place since the technician told us that she was a few weeks bigger than expected. Now, I can breathe." She sat up straight again, the lemonade sloshing in the glass. "How are you? With Demi moving out, I mean. This place is going to feel awfully big with just you in it."

Hera looked around at the twelve-foot ceilings, giant windows, and greenery everywhere. "I welcome all the space. Maybe I'll install silks from the ceiling. I've heard there are classes that you can take topside that will teach you how to twist yourself up in them and do acrobatic maneuvers."

"Why?" Chloe raised an eyebrow. "That sounds an awful lot like you're trying to distract yourself from being alone. Why don't you try an easier way of doing that by picking up a guy at Athens Bar?"

Hera wrinkled her nose. "No offence, but I'm not interested in the type that hang around at the bar. I know Achilles has been throwing pick-up lines at me for ages, so it would be a matter of snapping my fingers at him, but that's so *boring*!"

Chloe chuckled. "You want more of a

challenge?"

"A challenge and not clingy. I want a nice, reliable guy that will fuck me and leave afterward." Hera nodded decisively.

"You certainly don't make it easy, do you?" Chloe said, rubbing her belly as she thought. "If you wanted something long lasting, I would recommend—"

"Don't say it," Hera interrupted warningly. "Demi and Charles have been after me to try *speed dating* since your wedding." She shuddered and spat the words out as if they left a bad taste in her mouth. "I know that the one for this month is coming up in a couple days. The date's been mysteriously circled on every calendar in the apartment *and* the bakery."

"Okay, okay, I won't go there." Chloe raised her hands pacifyingly. "What about…" Chloe trailed off and tilted her head, examining Hera appraisingly.

"What?" Hera looked down at herself. She was wearing a simple work robe. It had a few tendrils of plants left on it from her time in the lab. She flicked them off impatiently. "What?" she asked again.

"How do you feel about Valhalla's Throne?" Chloe asked.

Hera paused. "The fight club?" She was about to shake her head dismissively, but caught herself. She rarely frequented that area of Purgatory; the area was gritty and dank. But the types of people, of supernatural beings, that would attend such a place would be vastly different from the patrons of Athens Bar. "I hadn't considered it, to be honest."

"Odin owns the place. I can get you in tonight, if you want. Go by. Check out the clientele. You might be able to scratch that itch with one of his men." Chloe smirked. "And then, you can think about settling down with someone later this week."

"Chloe!" Hera wouldn't say she whined, but it was a near thing. "You know I'm not the best judge of character."

"If you're talking about tonight, that doesn't matter. You just have to pick a guy that'll show you a good time. And Eve and Aphrodite will have your back later this week. That's what they're *there* for!"

Hera sighed. "I'm *not* saying yes to later this week. But I am saying yes to the fight tonight, please."

Chloe bounced excitedly. "I'll find out tonight's password as soon as I can. You get dressed. Something sexy and sensual. I want all the details tomorrow!" She winked. "Or maybe the day after."

Hera pretended to be shocked. "I don't own anything sexy!"

Chloe pursed her lips. "Are you a Goddess or not? Surely you can make something between now and the start of the fight." She examined Hera again. "Maybe play up your eyes a bit, wear light greys and silvers. Ooh, purple would really make them pop! An underbust corset in royal purple over a silver off-the-shoulder blouse. That would seriously emphasize your assets." Chloe winked at her.

"Spoken by someone with small breasts," Hera said, rolling her eyes.

"Where's the support? I wouldn't be emphasizing, I'd be flashing everyone."

"Use some power to keep your shirt up and no one will know," Chloe said with a shrug. "Let's see, a black leather skirt with a slit as high up your thigh as you can without showing everything, and knee-high black leather buckled boots with a thick heel. It's the perfect outfit for you, you have to agree." She wiggled some more and leaned forward.

Hera thought about it for a minute. "It's certainly not my style, but I'm willing to try it."

Chloe clapped her hands and gestured. "Go on!"

"If you insist," Hera muttered. She stood and waved a hand over herself, manifesting the outfit Chloe had described onto her body.

"I am *good*," Chloe muttered, standing and walking around the Goddess. "Yes, this is perfect. The heels give you extra height, and your eyes look stunning. Highlight them with purple eye-shadow, and maybe even a purple lip. You're a knockout without even getting into the ring!" She chuckled at her own joke.

Hera walked over to a mirror hanging on one wall, the swing of her hips emphasized by the heels. "I look... So unlike me," she breathed. She twisted, her heel popping up as she did so. "I like it."

***

Valhalla's Throne was in a dark and ominous area of town. The neon lights on the nearby clubs and bars all shone brightly in the gloom, announcing to the world that they were open for business.

Hera turned and descended the stairs to the metal door. There was a sliding grate just above her eye level. She tapped out the quick rhythm that Chloe had taught her before she left that evening, hoping she remembered it correctly.

The grate opened and a brown eye peered out at her.

Hera leaned up on her tiptoes and whispered, "Glaive."

The grate closed without a word from the person on the other side and Hera's heart sank into her leather boots. She was just about to turn away when the door creaked open. A wave of masculine musk wafted out, making Hera's knees weak. She wobbled a bit as she crossed the threshold into the dimly lit entry and held onto the wall for support.

"Right this way, miss," said the person with the brown eye. He only had one, right in the center.

Hera followed the Cyclops down the wood-paneled, dark-carpeted hallway and tried to regain her composure before there was the potential of an audience. The heavy velvet curtain at the end of the hall was held back for her, a wash of cheering, booing, and shouting crashing over her. "Thank you," Hera said and signed to the Cyclops in case he couldn't hear her over the noise.

He nodded and let the curtain fall behind her.

Excitement sang through her veins, more heady than a glass of ambrosia. She made a circuit of the room behind the spectator benches, made of natural logs that had been highly polished to a dark stain, looking for a likely target to bring home tonight.

A bell heralded the end of the match that was going on, an announcer joining the two fighters in the ring. Hera ignored them. She wasn't here for the fight. A tall, well-built older man with a full head of white-silver hair caught her eye, sitting in a private box the middle of the arena. Odin appeared absolutely regal as he lounged in a large seven foot chair carved of wood and depicting scenes from Norse Mythology, with his wolf and ravens surrounding him. He had a drink in one hand and an empty seat beside him.

With no fighters to make noise in the ring, Hera figured now was her chance.

Strutting over to the box, she tapped on the wooden side. "Excuse me," she said, enjoying the way his gaze traveled up her body. "Is that seat available?"

"I was saving it for you, milady," the man said, jumping to his feet and gesturing at the vacant spot on the bench beside his chair and offering her his right elbow.

She graciously accepted the aide of his arm as she squeezed past him to the seat. "Thank you most kindly, Odin," she said, feigning a slight stumble and pressing her breasts more fully against his hard chest. "I am pleased to make your acquaintance."

"I fear I am at a loss, milady, for you know my name, but I don't know yours."

Hera smiled at him, but her attention was quite suddenly drawn to the fighter's ring, where a large blond man had entered. His muscles were on full display, glistening under the lights. He wore only a pair of denim cut-offs. Her heart fluttered.

She turned her attention back to Odin. "Of course you know me. We met at Chloe and Lucifer's wedding. Chloe must have mentioned me and how it's my first time here. Now, tell me all about this fight club you initiated." She was suddenly quite interested in the fight.

# CHAPTER TWO

AUGUSTINE FLEW INTO the boards, and, since he was not shifted into his dragon form, crashed to the ground. He got to his feet and swiped a thumb across his lower lip, noting the blood that smeared across it. He spat into the sand that covered the fight ring and sneered at his opponent; a troll—literally. "Is that the best you have, you ructabunde?"

The insult made the crowd go wild, just as Augustine had intended. He was known as the Gentleman Fighter, always one with a quick insult that almost nobody understood. Today, he'd decided to utilize some of the lesser-known Greek insults. In this case, he'd called his opponent a gasbag.

"What did you call me?" growled the troll, his knuckles dragging on the ground as he readied to launch himself at Augustine.

"Would you prefer that I call you a quisquilian?" Augustine said, pretending to ignore the troll's attack cues. He sighed inwardly. Being brash wasn't really his style. He could put on a performance for the audience during a fight, but it was all an act.

The troll roared and charged at him,

picking him up by his thighs and dropping him over his back onto his head.

"Did not like that one either, huh?" Augustine gasped out. He'd called the troll worthless this time. He rolled out of the way, barely, as the troll attempted to throw himself elbow first toward Augustine's ribs. "That was rude."

The audience roared its approval as Augustine flipped onto his feet. He glanced at the clock. Only a few more minutes before the Ref would call the match. He knew what he had to do.

He caught sight of a stunning lady in purple high up in the audience sitting next to Odin. He wished she was closer so he could flirt with her. Instead, he leaned on the wall next to a pretty woman, all angular bones. Normally, she wouldn't draw his attention—he much preferred his women full-figured—but this wasn't about who turned him on. This was a way of flirting with the entire audience.

"My lady, that red compliments the crimson of your cheek," he said, winking at her. "I would wish that your cheeks blushed because of me." Augustine winced internally, hearing the double-entendre in his words after the fact.

The lady tittered, making his teeth ache, and offered her hand.

He kissed the back of it and smirked as the skin of her neck reddened. "If all your skin is this soft, I would have difficulty keeping my hands off of it."

The lady gasped and the back of Augustine's neck prickled. His instincts told him the troll was going to attack him while his back was turned.

His stomach churned as he ignored every instinct screaming at him to react *right now!*

Large arms tackled him around the waist, smashing him against the boards and jarring every bone in his body.

He pushed off the wall sharply, the momentum toppling the two men backward. Augustine scrambled around, making a show of trying to get on top of the troll to pin him to the sandy ground. Ultimately, he failed and ended up underneath the troll when the Ref called an end to the match.

Augustine dragged his body down the long stone hallway and pushed the large, solid wood door that opened into the lush individual room set aside for him and his brothers on nights they fought.

He shrugged off his clothes, letting them fall haphazardly onto the immaculate white bathroom floor and dragged a hand down his face, grimacing as he felt sand get into the abrasions in his skin.

*Shower first.*

*Then I'll call them.*

The hot water was a balm to his skin and he could already feel the smaller cuts knitting themselves back together. He dried himself with one of the big fluffy towels and then put Band-Aids over the two or three larger scrapes, mostly to avoid getting any lotion into them. That hurt like a... Well, it hurt a lot.

He dialed his brothers and put his phone on the desk, on speaker. It rang while he dug the bottle of lotion out of his bag. His pale skin already shone with a slight purple sheen in the bright white light over the mirror and the backs of his hands looked dry, the first indication that his scales were going to appear.

"Hey brother!" Finley's voice came over the phone. "How did your fight go tonight?"

Augustine grimaced. "I rolled a one before I went out."

In order to hide their strength, the three brothers would roll a dice before a match. If it landed on a one, they were to lose. Augustine hated those nights. It wasn't the pain; he healed quickly. It was the feigning ignorance of fighting techniques. He had years of fighting under his belt, not just here at Valhalla's Throne, and to have to act as though he didn't know how...

"Had to happen sooner or later!" That was Jaden's voice. He sounded like he was trying not to laugh. He'd rolled a one before his last two fights.

Augustine stuck his tongue out at the phone. "It is not my fault the dice likes me." He groaned as he rubbed the lotion into his thigh muscle. "Ouch. I hate losing."

"Too bad!" Finley said, and *he* was definitely laughing.

"I saw a woman here tonight..." Augustine trailed off, not sure why he mentioned her. He let a large dollop fall onto his palm and started working the lotion into his opposite shoulder. "How much lotion do we have left in storage?" he asked.

"Enough for a couple months," Finley replied. "More if we use it sparingly."

"We are going to have to order from Hera again," Augustine said. "I do not want to run out."

"Stop distracting us. What was this about a woman?" Jaden practically shouted. "Did she swoon at your feet?"

Augustine chuckled. "She did not. I barely saw her, but... I do not know. I felt drawn to her."

There was silence on the other end of the line.

"Did I lose you?" Augustine asked, leaning forward to look at his screen.

"Yeah, you lost us when you said that this woman turned your head," Jaden teased.

Finley added, "What was so special about her?"

Augustine thought for a minute about the woman. She'd been sitting with Odin in the top row of the audience, wearing something vibrant purple and voluptuous. "I am not sure. Something about the way she was sitting, I guess."

"The way she was sitting?" Jaden burst into loud guffaws. "Oh brother, you have got to get laid!"

"Laid? Like sleeping?" Augustine asked, confused. He put the cap back on the lotion bottle and looked around the tiny room for his clothing.

"Yes, like sleeping," Finley said with a snort. "As in sleeping *with* a woman? Sex?"

"Right." Augustine blushed even though his brothers couldn't see him. He started yanking on his pants. "Maybe I should try to find a mate."

There was silence on the line again.

Augustine ignored it and hopped a bit

as he pulled up his jeans. "You do not think I should." It wasn't a question.

"I just..." Jaden trailed off uncertainly.

"Remember what happened last time," Finley whispered.

Augustine's fingers slipped on his zipper. "I think they have changed. The supernatural community is a lot more accepting of all sorts of races now. Why not," he lowered his voice to a whisper, "dragon shifters?"

"And if they're not?" Finley sounded angry now. Augustine was getting whiplash from the emotional outbursts. "What if they try to—? I don't want to be put to sleep for millennia again!"

"That would not happen." Augustine was fairly certain of that. "Are you saying that I am going to recklessly endanger you? You know I would not do that."

A knock on the door interrupted them.

"Hang on," Augustine said to his brothers. He opened the door to see an attendant. "Can I help you?" he asked apprehensively.

"I have a message for you," the man replied curtly. "I was told to wait for a response."

Heart pounding hard, Augustine took the plain white envelope and opened it. He expected to see a threatening letter; his brothers had put the idea of persecution into his mind and it was hard to shake.

*Gentleman Fighter,*

*Your bout was the only fight that drew my attention. I couldn't help but gape in awe at your body and how it moved around the ring. How it could move over me. I would very much like to get to know you better between my sheets. Please don't leave me waiting.*

The letter was signed with a stylized capital H and a dark purple lipstick stain.

Augustine realized that his jaw was hanging open and snapped it shut. "Does this kind of thing happen often?" he asked the attendant. Not waiting for an answer, he scrawled a quick response on the back of the letter. "Thank you," he said, and the man bowed slightly and left.

"What was that all about?" Jaden asked.

"Ugh, can you believe that I just got propositioned?" Augustine growled out. "By some woman who described me like a piece of meat!" It was probably the woman he'd flirted with near the end of the match.

*I really should not have done that.*

His brothers burst into laughter. "So, I take it you turned her down?"

"Of course I did! She does not know me." Augustine pulled on his shirt. He glanced at himself in the mirror, noticing his normally blue eyes of his human form were turning violet. He took a deep breath and forced his shift back, deep under his skin where it couldn't be found. "I am going to go to the Athens Bar tonight. Do not wait up."

"All right. Take care, Auggie," Finley said.

"Yeah, yeah." Augustine made a face at the phone after he hung up. His brothers meant well, but they were a tad overprotective. He did up the buttons on his shirt quickly.

*They might be free from the witch's curse that put us to sleep under the mountain, but they are not really* living.

He gathered the rest of his things in his duffel and headed out the back door of Valhalla's Throne to avoid the crowds. Or more importantly, to avoid the sender of that note.

Granted, Augustine hadn't dated in a very long time—millennia—but even so, he was *not* a...

What was the phrase?

An end table?

He shook his head as he stalked down the street.

*A one-night stand.*

Even the phrase made the hair on the back of his neck prickle. He craved the connection with a woman, something that could not be rushed. Besides that, he couldn't risk his dragon shifter status showing up in the midst of a passionate encounter with someone he didn't trust one hundred percent.

The loud music and bright lights of Athens Bar drew him like a moth to a flame. Augustine soon found himself sitting at the polished bar with a drink in hand. He felt the tension leave his back muscles after he'd drained half the pint and he was finally able to tune into the conversations around him.

"Do you think we should allow more humans in?"

"I'm not sure... They would have to be thoroughly vetted beforehand. They won't all turn out to be as accepting as Charles."

"But if we did, we'd really be opening up the dating pool in Purgatory."

"Do we really need to? Lucifer and Chloe didn't need a human, and you can see how happy they are together."

"But Demi would never have met her mate if Sharon hadn't meddled and sent a human."

Intrigued by the conversation, Augustine turned around on his bar stool and leaned backward against the solid wood. The two were both stunningly beautiful women, one dark and one fair.

The dark-haired one continued, "What kind of vetting are we talking about here? Personal recommendations from our people living topside?"

"To start." The blonde nodded her agreement. "We can discuss further expansion if that goes well."

"Maybe every second month can be a human-inclusive night. We should also put a little more effort into pushing it down here."

Augustine suddenly found two pairs of stunning blue eyes fixed on him. The blonde smiled at him, her sharp teeth glinting in the lights behind the bar.

"Hello, honey, have you heard about our speed dating nights?"

"Speed dating? No, I do not think so," Augustine said, suddenly feeling cornered even though the two women hadn't left their seats.

"Don't worry, dear, we don't bite," the brunette said. "Well, not without consent." She winked. "I'm Aphrodite, and this is Eve."

*Aphrodite.*

Augustine swallowed hard.

*I know that name.*

*Who doesn't?*

*The Goddess of love.*

"Pleased to meet you both," he said formally.

"So polite," cooed Eve. "So handsome. We could use more men like you at our speed dating event. You'd meet your mate quickly there."

Augustine looked from her to Aphrodite. "You have had many successes?"

She nodded, her eyes sharp as she looked at him.

He squirmed.

*What is she looking for?*

*Can she see what I am?*

"I am not sure how comfortable I am with something so fast. I have not dated in… a while."

"Then this is the perfect way to get your feet wet!" Eve exclaimed. She rose gracefully from her chair and plucked a business card from her purse. Her hips swayed as she walked over to him. "No expectations. You'll meet a bunch of women, and if you don't want to get to know any of them better, you can simply leave." She slid the business card into his shirt pocket and patted it, fingers lingering on his pectoral. "But I guarantee there'll be at least one that will strike your fancy."

"Thanks," Augustine croaked. The card felt like it was burning a hole in his dress shirt, or perhaps, that was simply her touch. Rather than watch Eve walk back to the table, he returned his gaze to Aphrodite. "When is it? I cannot go if it interferes with my business."

Aphrodite smiled. "Tomorrow night. It's at DeLux Cafe. Do you know where that is?"

He nodded. "There will not be humans there tomorrow, will there?" Telling a human that he was a dragon shifter seemed even more unmanageable than telling a resident of Purgatory.

"Unlikely." She raked her gaze over him and raised an eyebrow. "I can't imagine anyone having a problem with you, though."

Augustine blushed and changed the subject. "I will rearrange my schedule. Thank you, ladies." He swigged back his beer and got to his feet, ducking to avoid banging his head on one of the lower chandeliers. "See you tomorrow night."

"You won't regret it," Aphrodite called

after him.

He adjusted his duffel and set off for home.

*I hope she is right.*

*What will Finley and Jaden think?*

He found himself thinking about the beauty in the back of the audience at the fight club again. He'd never seen her before and wondered if that was due to his inattention or if it was really her first time at Valhalla's Throne.

*I could go back and ask Odin, but what does it matter?*

*I am not going to stalk the poor woman!*

He daydreamed the rest of the walk back to the outskirts of Purgatory and his brothers.

# CHAPTER THREE

HERA WOKE UP in as bad a temper as she had fallen asleep. The storm that filled Purgatory's skies was visible proof of her foul mood. She grumbled along with the thunder as she got dressed and headed downstairs to the bakery.

Demi was already hard at work in the kitchen, her apron dusted with flour from whatever treats she was making that day.

Hera sniffed the air. "Cinnamon?" she asked.

"Apple turnovers," Demi replied. She nodded to a stool she had pulled over to the counter. "Based on the weather this morning, you need some serious sister bonding time."

"No, I don't." Hera took the offered seat and bit into an icing sugar-dusted pastry. She moaned as the sweet tartness burst across her tongue. "Okay, that almost makes up for last night. Give me a bushel of these, please."

Demi laughed. "Not until you tell me what happened."

Hera groaned, not in pleasure this time.

"If you insist on broadcasting your emotions and half-drowning all of Purgatory, then I'm entitled to ask why."

Demi kneaded the ball of dough in front of her with a series of punches that made Hera wince.

"It's silly," Hera said.

"Obviously it isn't, since your state of mind is in such turmoil," Demi pointed out.

"I went to Valhalla's Throne last night," Hera blurted out. She bit her lip. "I wanted to find someone to bring home last night so I wouldn't be alone."

"Oh, honey," Demi cried out. "I'm sorry. This has all been so abrupt for you. Would you like me to sleep over tonight?"

"What?" It took Hera a second to realize why Demi was offering that. "No, no, that's not what... I meant *alone*." She wiggled her eyebrows meaningfully. "A girl's got needs, you know. You're lucky

Charles satisfies yours."

Demi blushed. "Oh. Yes. Quite." She cleared her throat. "You didn't find anyone worthy of your time?"

Hera rolled her eyes. "There were plenty of prospects. I could have brought Odin himself home, if I'd asked. He was giving all the right signals." She sighed. "But one of the fighters caught my eye, hook, line, and sinker."

"Oh, do tell!" Demi clapped her hands together, clouds of flour forming in the air. "What did he look like?"

"Muscles. Lots of them. All that golden skin on display, except for some cut-off jean shorts. Hair like a wheatfield in the midst of summer. As fast and as strong as an Olympian." Hera's eyes unfocused as she mentally pictured the fighter moving about in the ring. He had danced around his larger opponent with feet as light as feathers, landing blows that she could feel in her chest.

And then he'd flirted with some woman in the front row.

Hera's blood boiled. Outside, a lightning bolt forked through the sky. Unbeknownst to her, her wings popped into existence, filling a quarter of the kitchen. Lost in her memories, she didn't notice Demi's squeak of dismay.

His flirtation had cost him his match and he had limped out of the ring while the fickle audience had applauded the troll.

Hera had left Odin and slipped off to the side, where she'd quickly written a letter to the handsome fighter, hoping that she could be balm to his wounded soul. She desperately needed to feel his hips between her thighs. Perhaps his shoulders, too, at some point during the evening. She'd signed it with her initial and lipstick print and sent it off with an attendant.

The resulting answer had crushed her faster than she thought possible.

"I'm pretty, aren't I?" Hera asked Demi, giving herself a shake that brought her back to the present.

"Beautiful," Demi agreed readily.

"Desirable?"

Demi stopped making little rounds of dough and put her hands on her hips. "Of course you are." She called attention to Hera's wings. "Would you mind putting those away? I need to get the cinnamon and they're in the way."

"Oh, drat." Hera frowned and concentrated on calming herself down so that her wings would disappear. Once they did her bidding, she reached behind her back and felt the damage to her sweater. "Argh!"

Demi snapped her fingers and the shirt mended itself. "Still can't do that yourself?" She started shaking cinnamon into a new bowl of dough.

"Nope. I can't fix anything my wings have damaged," Hera grumbled.

"No matter. I'm here for you this time, but you really do need to go see Arachne and get some of her divine creations so you won't have that issue anymore." Demi turned to grab something else from the other side of the kitchen. "What's your plan now?"

Hera shrugged. "I've had lots of lovers," she said, half to herself. "None of them have ever left my bed unsatisfied.

Why does one man's rejection hurt so much?" Her words ended on a squeaky gasp that made her cringe.

Demi hugged her from the side and Hera rested her head on the comforting shoulder. "His rejection probably had nothing to do with you. Was he even single?"

Hera opened and closed her mouth. "You know, I have no idea." A tiny giggle escaped and she clapped a hand over her mouth. "My goodness, I can't believe I was so forward without even introducing myself!"

"There you go." Demi stroked Hera's hair softly. "Are you feeling better?"

"Where were you last night when I was in the depths of despair?" Hera groaned. "I feel so silly that I let this get to me!"

"You can call me any time, sister dear," Demi said. She pulled away and went to the sink to wash her hands. "I must finish these butter buns. Don't you have work to do?"

Hera wiped her eyes with the back of her hand. "Yes, I do. I'm taking this with me, though." She indicated the platter of apple turnovers.

Demi laughed. "They're all yours."

On the way to her office, Hera glanced out a window. The clouds had almost fully vanished from the sky and the sun was shining brightly. She nodded in satisfaction.

*That's better.*

The morning passed quickly, her nose buried in paperwork for ButterNut Bakery. Today was usually the day that she added up receipts, but she kept finding her mind wandering. By lunchtime, she'd done only half her usual amount of work, and she was frustrated with herself.

"Fine!" Hera said as she burst into the bakery where Demi was helping a customer. "I'll do it. I'll go."

It took Demi a moment, and then a huge grin broke across her face. "Really?" she squealed, clapping her hands together giddily. "Oh, we're going to have so much fun getting you ready!"

"No. I'm not going to dress up for this. I'm going to go wearing something that I'm comfortable in. If guys don't like me at my worst, they don't deserve me at my best," Hera said decisively.

"Oh, honey, no. Not your worst," Demi gasped with wide eyes.

Hera frowned. "Well, no, I suppose

not. But I'm not putting any extra effort into my appearance."

Demi pursed her lips. "All right. If you insist. I do see your point."

"I don't want guys who only want to bring me to bed. I'm looking for forever, and I don't want to be someone I'm not." Hera turned her gaze on the customer. "What do *you* think?"

The man looked uncomfortable. "I think you're right."

Hera snorted. "Spoken like someone with a wife." She turned back to Demi. "My man needs to be able to disagree with me."

"Why would I disagree if you're right?" the man said timidly.

Demi handed him his receipt with a smile. "You should probably go."

"Right." He took his bag and hurried

out the door.

Hera watched him go, amused. "Definitely more backbone than *that*. Someone who makes me laugh. I want chemistry, long-term. I want what you and Charles have."

"I'm sure you'll find it," Demi enthused. "Aphrodite and Eve are very good at what they do. Do you want me to go with you?"

"For moral support?" Hera chuckled. "No, thank you. I can handle this on my own."

"You'll call me the minute you get home and tell me all about it, won't you?" Demi asked.

Hera raised an eyebrow. "What, like you did?"

Demi blushed. "I did tell you. Eventually."

"All right." Hera took a sandwich from behind the glass case. "I'll tell you tonight. Or tomorrow morning when we're setting up the bakery, at the latest." She smiled. "I might be too tired tonight to call you."

"Hera!" Demi pretended to be shocked, but Hera could tell she wasn't. Not really.

"I've got a lot to do in the apothecary this afternoon," Hera said, her skirt floating about her legs as she twirled away from the case. "See you at closing!"

"Remember that it starts at eight sharp tonight!" Demi called after her. "Don't get so caught up in your work that you forget to get ready!"

"Don't worry, I won't show up in my lab coat," Hera teased.

She returned to her office with her

sandwich, energy refocused. She finished the accounts in record time, tidied up, and headed upstairs to her apartment and the lab. She had picked several herbs a couple days ago that should be dry by now, and she set about crushing and mixing them with drops of various different oils.

By dinnertime, Hera had a tidy row of bottles ready to be delivered over the next few days to the customers who had ordered them. She checked her list of orders and made a mental note to work on the shifter-masking potion the next day.

*Must be someone who works topside.*

The absentminded thought flitted through her head and then she promptly forgot about it as she strolled into her room to get ready for her evening out.

Hera headed for her closet, perusing her options. She settled on a one-shouldered dress in a jade green. It had bronze brocade work gathering the material on her left shoulder and under her bust. The skirt floated around her legs when she walked.

When she joined Demi at the table in the dining room, she was assessed appraisingly.

"When you said you weren't going to put any effort in, I was worried," Demi said. She nodded slowly. "But this... I see what you mean. You've worn this to work in the garden, to go shopping, to visit friends. It's not fancy, but it is very *you*. Are you going to put on any make-up?"

"Do you think I need to?" Hera asked challengingly.

"No." Demi speared a bite of potato on her fork. "Stop attacking me. Sometimes you wear it. I was *asking*."

"Sorry." Hera sat and picked at the food on her plate, pushing it around. "I figure if this mythical guy is going to see me in the mornings before I get out of bed, he should know what to expect, right? I mean, do you apply mascara before Charles wakes up?"

Demi snorted with laughter. "Of course not."

"Exactly. And getting all sweaty with the guy will be even less attractive—well, besides the fact that we're, you know, doing it—so he might as well see the real me right away." Hera took a bite of chicken and moaned her appreciation. "Delicious, Demi. Thank you for making dinner."

"I knew that if I didn't, you wouldn't remember to eat." Demi rolled her eyes fondly.

"Sure I would have," Hera protested, but she knew her sister was right. "I might have grabbed a bun or something." She changed the subject to avoid chastisement. "I'm actually looking forward to tonight."

"That's a great attitude to have! It's not the end of the world if you don't find your soulmate tonight. Just have fun and enjoy the conversations you have." Demi waggled an asparagus at Hera in admonition. "Don't get all caught up in your head."

It was on the tip of Hera's tongue to argue that she never did that, but she knew that was a lie. Instead, she nodded and continued her meal in deep thought.

*You have nothing to lose tonight.*
*You can do this.*

With that thought in mind, Hera finished her meal and then made her way down the street to the cafe.

"I'm here for the speed dating?" she informed the bouncer, who let her in with barely a glance.

The entry from Purgatory was on the same level as the speed dating event. Hera knew that there was an upper part of the cafe topside for humans, but she wasn't interested in that part today.

"Hera! You made it!"

Hera recognized the sultry voice of Eve before she saw the blonde vampire bent over behind the desk. "There are still a few minutes before it starts, aren't there?"

"Yes, of course." Eve sat up and

handed her a ballot and a pen. "Please sign in and we'll get you organized. I believe you're the last person to arrive tonight so the evening will start after you've—ah, thank you." She plucked the ballot from Hera's fingers and put it in a box. "Right this way."

She'd never been inside Lucifer's celebrated cafe before tonight. The coffered ceilings were high, with elegant golden candelabras that illuminated the space. The walls were covered in a rich, woven wallpaper with mahogany beams as accents. Leather chairs were arranged around round wooden tables, one on each side so that the participants could see each other while they chatted on their speed date.

Aphrodite swooped in and escorted Hera to a table at the side. "You're just in time to be the last person seated. I thought we might end up with an uneven number tonight!" She gave Hera's shoulders a gentle push.

Hera found herself seated across from a short, thin man. He smiled at her, but she didn't have time to offer one in return before Aphrodite started speaking to the room of people.

"You have five minutes to date your partner before the men switch tables. You'll be given ten seconds to mark down your compatibility on your ballots before you start your new date. Any questions?" Aphrodite paused, looking around the room for raised hands. "You may begin!" She rang a little bell.

The man turned back to face Hera and clasped his hands on the table. "Good evening, my name is Cliff. I would like to begin by saying that you look lovely tonight."

"Thank you. I'm Hera."

The little man jumped. "As in the Goddess? Zeus's paramour?" He looked nervously around the room.

Hera sighed. "Yes, the Goddess. I have never dated Zeus and never plan to. I hate that rumor."

Cliff didn't seem convinced and the rest of their date was filled with stilted conversation. Hera almost cheered when the bell sounded and Cliff left her table. She marked down a zero next to his number before looking up at the next person to sit down in front of her.

"Hello, I'm Kurtis. You shine more radiant than the sun. Have you heard about the dragon shifters appearing?"

*Oh boy.*

# HERA

*Will they all be like this?*

*Empty compliments and rumors?*

Suddenly, the night didn't seem quite as fun.

# CHAPTER FOUR

AUGUSTINE WANTED TO groan with frustration. He had been on two dates so far, both with women he was sure were delightful, but he kept saying things that completely confused them. He had never felt so disconnected to the world. Certainly, speaking with Odin hadn't proved to be this difficult.

*I should try out some of the conversation topics my brothers came up with for the next date.*

*Maybe that would help.*

He pulled back his chair at the next table, where an ogre was sitting. "Good evening, I am Augustine. Pleased to make your acquaintance."

"I'm Chantalle. Nice to meet you." The ogre had a high, breathy voice.

"I like your necklace," he said, nodding at the extraordinarily fancy and overdone piece of jewelry. "Does it have a story?"

"Oh, no, not really. It was a gift from my sister for my birthday a couple years ago." The ogre touched the dangling red gem closest to her cleavage provocatively.

"Are you close with your family?" Augustine appreciated strong family values.

*These questions are working nicely!*

He made a mental note to thank his brothers.

"I suppose so. We live in the same city!" Chantalle giggled and tossed her long blonde hair behind her shoulder.

"Have you lived in Purgatory long?"

"All my life. My ancestors were some of the original founders."

"Really? That is fascinating. Has it changed much since its inception?"

"Quite a bit, but more so in the last year, since our lord met his wife." She leaned forward, her low cut neckline threatening to expose her breasts. "She lived topside, you know."

"I had heard that," Augustine replied politely. "She is a shifter, correct?"

"A wolf shifter, yes." Chantalle began to frown, her prominent brow furrowing.

"Are shifters not... accepted here?" Augustine asked hesitantly.

Chantalle crossed her arms. "Of course they're accepted. Why wouldn't they be?"

Augustine realized he'd spent most of their date talking about another woman and mentally chastised himself. "What do you do for a living?" he asked, changing the subject.

"I am a seamstress," Chantelle said. "I made this myself." She stood up to show off the form-fitting gold-lamé sheath dress. It rode high on the thigh and low on the breasts, making Augustine wonder if she ever had problems with it rolling up in the middle.

"You do beautiful work," he complimented her abilities, reminding himself he was being polite despite the fact he'd seen far better at that new place in town. What was it called? *Metamorphosis*. Yes, that was it. "What else have you made recently?"

That set her off on a long monologue about different fabrics and patterns she had used recently, throwing around sewing terms that went completely over his head. He breathed a mental sigh of relief when the date was over, moving on to the next table after a bow to Chantalle.

The scent of vanilla and apple pie hit him before he saw the woman's face, overwhelming his senses. Then she smiled at him and his heart almost stopped beating.

*Get a hold of yourself and don't scare this one off.*

"Evening, my name is Augustine."

"I'm Hera." She held out a dainty hand and he kissed the back of it.

"I like your n—" He glanced at her neck, but she wasn't wearing jewelry.

*Neck?*

*No, I am not a vampire.*

*Nose?*

*That sounds weird.*

*I have been staring too long!*

*Say something!*

"Eyes," he finished and cringed inwardly.

Hera looked amused. "You like my *neyes*?"

"Can I start over?" Augustine covered his burning cheeks with his hands. "That did not come out right at all!"

"What were you trying to say?"

He saw only amusement in her eyes, no malice, so he took a deep breath. "My brothers helped me come up with conversation topics because it has been a while since I last dated. That was my attempt at saying that I liked your necklace, but you are not wearing one. And then I panicked," he finished sheepishly.

"That's quite all right. It's been a while since I dated, too." She leaned forward. "And I'm nervous as well. You have brothers?"

"Two of them." His embarrassment fading, her name finally filtered through. "Wait, you are Hera?"

Her expression shuttered. "Yes."

"As in Hera's Potions and Lotions?"

"Oh!" She smiled brightly at him. "Yes, that's me."

"I use your lotion every day. It is amazing." Augustine rolled back the royal blue sleeve of his dress shirt to his elbow and offered Hera his wrist to sniff.

Her eyes widened as she smelled the lotion he had used before getting dressed.

And then beautiful white-feathered wings popped into existence behind her. A sound of tearing material met his ears, but before he could figure out what that meant, Hera gave a squeaking gasp and clutched the material of her dress to her chest.

Augustine immediately reached behind him for his coat, draping it over her chest. "Are you all right?"

Hera blinked her big grey eyes up at him for a moment before she started to laugh.

He sat back down, a little confused. "Was it something I said?"

"No, no," she managed to say through her giggles. "It's just... These *wings*! I can't control them at all—" They fluttered as if in agreement and knocked over a potted plant nearby. They had an impressive wingspan, almost reaching to the table next to them where Chantalle was sitting with her date. He couldn't help but want to compare them to his own wings. The white would look beautiful next to the purple scales of his dragon form.

"And whenever they rip my clothes, I can't fix them."

Augustine was confused for a minute. "With needle and thread? Do they destroy that much of your clothing?"

"I'm a Goddess. I can usually use my powers, but—"

Aphrodite hurried over to them. "I'm

sorry, I couldn't help but notice your—" She gestured at Hera. "Distress. Can I help?" She held up her fingers.

"Please," Hera said. "Hang on a minute. If I can calm down, they usually go away." She closed her eyes and took a couple deep breaths and the wings disappeared. She opened her eyes again. "Now, please."

Aphrodite snapped her fingers.

"Thank you very much."

"Not a problem, honey," Aphrodite said. She moved away.

"You cannot fix them?" Augustine snapped his fingers, imitating Aphrodite.

"Exactly." Hera flailed with her hands, making him smile. "Anyone else can, but I can't. It's like my lotions and other potions. They work on everyone else *except* for me. Just a tiny bit frustrating. More so now that my sister's gone to live topside."

"Did you live with your sister?"

"Yes, I did. Are you close with your brothers?"

"I do. I live with them. What do you do, when you are not making incredible lotions?" Augustine wanted to know everything about this amazing woman in front of him.

"I work in the back of ButterNut Bakery."

"You bake, too?"

"Oh, no, definitely not!" Hera laughed again. "I meant with the books. What about you? What do you do?"

Ah, the million dollar question. He couldn't very well say that he was an underground fighter. "I work in sports entertainment," he said, using the line that he and his brothers had come up with for just this sort of scenario.

"That's exciting! You must have lots of stories to tell. What sort of sport?"

The bell rang then, startling them both.

"I guess our time's up," Hera said.

Augustine hoped she was disappointed, although he was glad her questions about his job had been derailed. "I will come find you after the dates?"

Hera smiled. "Yes, please."

*Yes!*

Augustine shot her a smile. "Should I leave my jacket with you in case of further accidents?"

"I don't think it will happen again," Hera replied with a wink. "It only seems to happen when I'm incredibly flustered or stressed."

"I hope your reaction to me was not stress?" Augustine asked.

"I assure you, it was the opposite of stressed," Hera replied demurely.

A man clearing his throat from beside Augustine distracted him and he leapt to his feet. "My lady," he said with a bow as he moved away to the next table, not even glancing at the man taking his place.

The rest of the dates passed by in a blur of faces and names that he didn't bother to remember. Every time he switched between dates, he would look back at Hera, only to find her gaze on him. He didn't write anything further on his ballot, just circling her number and putting a '10' next to it. On his next switch, he added her name just in case he'd remembered her number wrong.

At the end of the dates, he double-checked his ballot before it was collected by Eve.

She glanced at the back and smirked up at him. "Just the one, then?"

"Yes," he said emphatically. He lowered his voice to not offend any of the other ladies, "Nobody else holds a candle to her."

"You really hit it off, didn't you?" Eve said.

"Hit?" Augustine was confused for a moment. "Oh, you mean we got along. Yes, for my part. She also seemed inclined."

Eve smiled mysteriously. "You'll find out."

Augustine bowed to her and pivoted slightly to peruse the room. He was in a slightly shadowy corner, so nobody seemed to notice him and he was able to take his time. There were several men with groups of women surrounding them and multiple men by themselves nursing beers. Augustine winced in sympathy for those men. He couldn't see Hera anywhere, though.

Moving out of his corner slightly, he saw her at one edge of the bar. The broad back of one of the men had hidden her from his view before. She was leaning back as far as she could manage in the tight space he allowed her and kept her drink between them. Everything about her body language screamed discomfort at her situation.

*What should I do?*

*Let her handle this or step in?*

He made his way across the room,

avoiding making eye contact with the other women, until he was directly behind the big man.

Hera's wide grey eyes met his and she smiled, relieved.

"*There* you are, August," she said, slipping off her stool and sidestepping the man. "I was hoping we could play a game of darts, just you and me?"

Augustine's brain rebooted after the affectionate nickname she had bestowed upon him. "Of course," he said graciously, offering her his arm and leading her over to the dartboards. Once they were out of earshot, he said, "Do you want to play darts or were you just that desperate to get away from him?"

"A little of both," Hera said with a chuckle that ended in a sigh. "How's your game?"

"Terrible," he said, deadpan. "My brothers and I have a board set up in our living room. It is all we do on our days off."

"I don't know if you're joking or not," Hera said, picking up her first dart. "I guess I'll find out soon enough." The dart hit one of the single areas and she wiggled her body excitedly. "I hit the board!"

"Yes, you did." Augustine let his first dart fly, hitting the bullseye.

"You are very good," Hera said. "I'm impressed. First one to reach a score of two-hundred and one gets to pick the first date?"

Augustine grinned. "You are on. First toss counts."

Hera frowned but agreed. Her second dart hit the triple ring under the '20'.

"Did you try to hustle me?" he asked, eyebrows rising. His next dart hit the bullseye again.

"We both win no matter what," Hera replied archly. Her third hit the same triple ring as the last one.

"That is true." Augustine lined up his third dart. There was barely enough room for it when it hit the bullseye again.

"Nicely done," Hera replied. Her fourth dart joined the other two in the same space.

"You are very good at this," Augustine said admiringly. "But I have a hundred and fifty points. I only need one more bullseye and then I can take my pick of the board to pass two-hundred."

"You're right," Helen replied serenely. "Go ahead."

Augustine frowned in concentration as he aimed at the board. There was a tiny space in the middle of his cluster that he needed to hit. He released a breath and the dart at the same time, his aim true.

"Beautiful," Hera replied. Her fifth dart joined the other three in the triple ring. "But I've won."

"Wait... What?" Augustine blinked.

"I passed two hundred. Twenty times three, for the triple ring, times four, for the four darts, makes two-hundred and forty." Hera's expression was entirely too smug.

Augustine closed his jaw, not sure when it had opened. She was right. "Do not forget the sixteen from your first throw," he finally added. "Even if I somehow managed to get another bullseye, I would not be able to pass your score. Congratulations, my lady. I concede defeat. You are incredibly clever and I consider it an honor to be schooled so soundly by you."

Hera beamed up at him. "You can tell a lot about a man by how he loses to a woman. That was quite gracious."

"I am kicking myself for not doing the math properly before we started, believe me," Augustine said ruefully. "I will not make the same mistake again."

"I expect not!" Hera said with a chuckle. "Will you walk me home?"

"I would love to," Augustine said. "Shall I fetch your coat?"

"I didn't bring one," Hera replied.

"Then you may have mine," he offered immediately, draping it around her shoulders.

"Won't you be cold?"

"I run warm," Augustine reassured her, trying not to feel too possessive. She looked so tiny in his large jacket.

"Leaving so soon?" Eve asked them at the door. "You're not interested in your matches?"

Hera smiled and squeezed Augustine's arm. "I've found mine, thank you. No others are necessary."

"That is excellent news." Eve's smile showed all her teeth, including two razor sharp eyeteeth, making Augustine shiver a tiny bit.

He wasn't quite sure what they talked about on the short walk to ButterNut Bakery, but suddenly they were standing in front of her door.

"Would you like to come up?" Hera asked, linking their fingers as she turned to face him.

Augustine swallowed hard. "I would like to, but I am going to have to decline. I am not sure I would be able to control myself around you in a private setting."

"What if that's what I want?" Hera pressed her body against his.

His fingers twitched as he wrapped his arms around her tiny body. "I am not ready to take that step, yet. Please do not be offended. It is a big deal for me and I wish to get to know each other better before we fall into bed together."

Hera smiled up at him. "I can take things slow. You're worth it. May I have your number? I would like to be able to reach you to plan our first date."

Augustine pulled his cell phone out of his back pocket and handed it to her unlocked. She gave him hers and he quickly typed in his name and number.

"Good night, August." Hera slipped out of his coat and handed it back to him. "I'll talk to you soon."

"Good night, Hera." He kissed the back of her hand, getting a whiff of vanilla and apple pie again. "Sweet dreams."

He waited until she had entered her apartment before he shrugged into his coat, her scent on the collar filling his senses. Thoughts of her accompanied him the entire way home.

# CHAPTER FIVE

"IS IT *THAT* bad?"

Hera gave herself a mental shake, dragging her mind back to the present and her sister, who was looking upset. "Sorry, something's bad?"

"The apple tart!"

"Ooooh you made an apple tart?" Hera sniffed the air. "Where?"

Demi huffed, exasperated. "Beside you on the counter."

Hera's mouth dropped open. "I didn't even notice it!"

"You didn't—" Demi cut herself off and snapped her fingers. The tart was suddenly steaming slightly, refreshed. "Try it, and then you simply must tell me about this guy that has got you daydreaming for *hours*!"

"Surely, it hasn't been that long," Hera protested, glancing at the clock on the wall of the kitchen. "Oh no! I have to finish up that shifter-masking lotion today or else the herbs will be useless!"

"Don't think you're getting out of telling me about your night!" Demi called after her. "I'll see you at dinner!"

"See you!" Hera replied, taking the stairs up to her apartment two at a time. She went immediately to her lab, pulling out the lavender and sandalwood that she hadn't used the day before. The sandalwood was now sufficiently dried that she could crush it for use in her lotion.

As she used her mortar and pestle, her thoughts drifted back to Augustine the night before. She hadn't needed him to tell her that he used her lotion; the minute he'd been close enough, she could smell it. His natural musk with the sandalwood had been a mixture that had gone straight to her head—and other places.

She shivered, her sense-memory taking hold as the delicious aroma of the spicy wood filled the air. The soft skin of his inner wrist had been a surprise and contrasted with the strength she could feel running through his muscles. Her knees felt weak and she gripped the edge of her workbench to steady herself.

A crash broke through her reverie and Hera realized her wings had popped into existence again, this time knocking over glassware and dried herbs. "Drat! Is this going to happen every time I get too excited by that man?" She stomped a foot in frustration, glass crunching under her shoe.

She rolled her eyes and took several deep breaths, focusing on one of the ferns in the main living space. A whoosh of air, and the feathered monstrosities were gone. She heaved a sigh of relief and surveyed the damage. Another roll of her eyes and a snap of her fingers whisked all the broken glassware back onto the shelves behind her, their contents restored.

She ignored the damage to the back

of her shirt and lab coat. Demi would fix them later.

Her phone dinged in her pocket.

*Thinking about you. Looking forward to our date this Saturday.*

Hera felt butterflies in her abdomen and wondered if he was thinking about her the way she was thinking about him.

She fired off a quick reply and attempted to focus on her work.

***

"Tell me everything," Demi said while they were making dinner. "What were the men like?"

Hera snorted. "Most of them were ridiculous. One of them tried to tell me he'd seen dragon shifters flying around Purgatory, can you believe it?"

"Seriously? How does that even come

up on a date?" Demi asked with a chuckle.

"He led with it. After an empty compliment." Hera stirred the sauce more vigorously. "I guess it was a unique approach. Certainly memorable."

"Dragon shifters," Demi mused. "I haven't seen one of those in, well, ages!"

"Weren't they supposed to be evil?" Hera asked.

"So were humans," Demi said scornfully. "You and I both know that you can't tar an entire race with the same brush, if you pardon the idiom."

"Good point," Hera agreed. "I had no idea they were still around."

"The story, as far as I can remember, goes that the witches put the last of the dragon shifters to sleep deep in the Earth," Demi said musingly.

"If that's true, why would they be waking up now?" Hera wondered out loud.

"There was that earthquake a few months ago," Demi suggested. "It's possible that woke them." She laughed. "Or maybe their hibernation period was done."

Hera laughed with her sister and bumped their hips. "Or maybe he simply saw an eagle and mistook it for a dragon."

"Far more likely." Demi nodded sagely, sending them off into giggles again. "But in all seriousness, what has got you daydreaming? Or should I say whom?"

Blushing, Hera started plating the pasta. "There was one man... Demi, he was amazing!"

"Do tell!"

"He was extremely awkward, and it was so adorable. His brothers helped him come up with conversation topics and his opening line was supposed to be to compliment my jewelry, but I wasn't wearing any." Hera giggled.

"Oh no, that poor boy," Demi gasped, pasta sauce dripping unheeded off her spoon onto the counter. "So, what did he do?"

"He stumbled over his words and complimented my eyes." Hera cleaned the counter with a snap of her fingers and continued, "He's a shifter, although, we didn't talk about what kind. He uses my lotion to mask his characteristics."

"What's his name?" Demi asked, getting the sauce onto the plate this time.

"Augustine. I called him August. He didn't tell me not to, but I should really ask him if he's okay with his name being shortened," Hera said thoughtfully. Then she remembered the swooping, swoony feeling she'd gotten... "When my wings appeared, he didn't even flinch."

"Your wings?" Demi asked, surprised. "He really affected you, didn't he?"

"You have *no* idea," Hera said emphatically, picking up her plate and fork and carrying them to the table.

"How was the kiss?" Demi followed her example.

"Non-existent."

Demi's jaw dropped. "You're kidding."

"I'm not. He kissed the back of my hand, but he said he didn't want to come upstairs. That he didn't trust himself around me in private and that he wants to wait." Hera sighed heavily.

"Well..." Demi dragged it out. "Maybe he's the kind of person who wants to get to know their partner before having sex. That's not exactly a bad thing, especially considering you went to the speed dating event looking for Mister Forever, right?"

"That is an excellent point," Hera said, wagging her fork at her sister. "I'm not upset by it. Obviously. Look at the skies."

Demi chuckled. "That's true. What's the plan? When is your first date? Where is he taking you?"

"*I* am taking *him* out on Saturday afternoon. I'm going to fill a picnic basket and we're going to rent bicycles and ride along the beach in L.A.," Hera said.

"That sounds awesome! Where did

you get the idea?"

"He said he was in sports entertainment, so I figured that we should do something sporty. And you can't go wrong with a picnic, not with ButterNut Bakery sandwiches." Hera wiggled in satisfaction. "I won at darts, so I got to plan the first activity."

"How did he handle that?"

Hera nearly choked on her pasta as she recalled his expression. "He was so surprised!"

"But not angry?" Demi asked, concerned.

"No, definitely not that." Hera smirked. "I made sure of that. I didn't want to risk dating someone who can't handle losing."

"Good call," Demi said. "Not that you can't handle yourself."

"Obviously," Hera said with a chuckle. "But I'd still rather not be in that position."

"Nobody would," Demi agreed.

***

The rest of the week had passed at a snail's pace. Saturday dawned gloomy, but cleared along with Hera's mood as she drank her morning coffee. She chose a summery yellow sundress with red cherries dotted on it and paired it with pure white strappy sandals.

"You look lovely," Demi said admiringly as Hera entered the bakery with a picnic basket looped over one arm. "I made you some ham and swiss on ciabatta, which should hold well until you get to your picnic spot. I also wrapped up some spiced carrot cake for dessert and filled a thermos with lemonade.”

“You are the best,” Hera enthused. “Thank you so much.”

“Just don’t take credit for my hard work,” Demi said with a wink.

Hera put a hand to her breast. “I would *never*!” She filled the basket quickly. “I’m off!”

They had agreed to meet up at the café, as it was the easiest and closest way to get topside. Augustine arrived at the same time as she did and smiled, offering her his arm and leading her through the café to Los Angeles.

The sun was still low, but the heat was already oppressive. Hera could feel the small of her back get sticky with sweat.

*Ugh, that’s attractive.*

A small snap of her fingers and she was cool again, like a mini air conditioning unit.

"Shall we find the bike rental shop?" she asked.

Augustine nodded and turned right, leading the way along the sidewalk. "It is near the boardwalk beside the beach. I checked it out on my run earlier this week," he finished, his face reddening.

"Good idea," Hera said brightly. "You must have been nervous." She grinned at his obvious shyness. "I was nervous, too," she added.

Augustine relaxed slightly. "Nice to know we are on the same page. Here we go."

The rental place was tucked in between a sandwich shop and a bathing suit store. They each picked out a bicycle, Augustine giving his dubious looks.

"Have you ridden a bike before?" Hera asked, sitting astride hers after stowing the picnic basket in front of her handlebars.

"Err, no," Augustine said sheepishly, running a hand through his blond hair.

Hera's fingers itched to follow the same path. "How's your balance?"

"Well enough, I suppose," Augustine said. He tried to copy her stance and his knee came up to his elbow. "Is this right?"

"Oh dear, I don't think that bike is quite big enough for your long legs," Hera said, trying not to giggle. He looked like he was sitting on a child's bike. "Why don't I see if they have something bigger."

They did not.

"I could run alongside you while you bike," Augustine suggested. "I am pretty fast."

"Or we could both walk," Hera pointed out. "There isn't exactly a lack of beach here."

"But you wanted to ride," Augustine protested. "I do not mind."

"I do." Hera returned both bikes. "There's a silver lining. This way we can talk without a problem."

Augustine took the picnic basket from her and offered her his elbow. "What would you like to talk about?"

"Why haven't you ridden a bicycle before?"

"I think we already saw the problem with that," he replied dryly and indicated his long legs. "Honestly, I like walking. I did not see the point of learning how to ride a bike. I do know how to ride a horse, though."

"Really?" Hera bounced a little in excitement as she walked. "I've always wanted to try that."

"I could take you next weekend, if you like," Augustine suggested. Then he coughed bashfully. "If today goes well."

"I think today is going swimmingly," Hera said, bumping her hip into his. "Oooh, I like that spot!" She pointed at a hollow near a copse of palms. "Just enough shade, but still plenty of sun."

"A perfect choice," Augustine agreed amiably.

"Oh drat, I forgot the blanket," Hera said, stomping her foot a little. "And there's too many people around for me to call it into existence."

"What if I reach into the basket and pull one out?" he said. "Make something that would fit in there."

Hera smiled. "Quick thinker." She snapped her fingers and Augustine pulled out a thin blanket. "We'll weigh the corners down with sand."

"Did you want to eat lunch right away or relax?" Augustine asked.

"I'm not hungry yet. Why don't we go for a walk at the edge of the water? Nobody will touch our things and we'll work up an appetite."

Plan decided on, they kicked off their shoes and left them on the blanket. Hera put up a shield around it and walked toward the water, the sand warm under her feet.

"I could get used to dating a Goddess," Augustine joked. "Those spells you do have been very useful.”

“Thank you.” Hera curtsied, small wavelets rippling about her ankles “I've gotten rather used to having access to them, I must admit. It's hard to be around humans. Or rather, humans that don't know.”

“Ah yes, your sister is dating a human, correct?” Augustine stayed out of reach of the water, walking in the wet sand.

“Yes. Charles. He's quite nice and Demi adores him,” Hera said. “I especially liked when he showed up at our doorstep with a bunch of—oh no!”

“A bunch of oh no?” Augustine frowned in confusion.

Hera tugged on his arm, turning him back the way they had come. “The food!”

“What about the food? I thought we

were talking about Charles.”

“He brought Demi a bouquet of flowers from topside. And when he brought them down to Purgatory, they all *died*!” Hera declared dramatically.

“What does that have to do with the food?” Augustine asked, obviously not following her train of thought.

“Living things like plants and food can’t be brought from one to the other. It rots! I can’t believe I forgot that, and Demi did, too!” Hera groaned.

“Oh no,” Augustine said, catching on.

They ran back to their picnic and opened the basket, peeking in. The stench was unbearable.

“How did we miss that when I pulled the blanket out?” Augustine asked, dismayed.

“The blanket wasn’t technically *in* the

basket. It only existed once it was out. And we closed it immediately afterward." Hera felt like crying. *Both* parts of her date were ruined.

"Hey, none of that," Augustine said, taking her face in his gentle, large hands. He swiped a thumb under one of her eyes and she realized that a tear had escaped. "I saw a sandwich shop back there. How about we go buy things that were similar to what you had planned."

"We don't have any money," Hera sniffed.

"How were you going to pay for the bicycle rentals?"

"Oh. Right."

Augustine chuckled. "I am going to get rid of this—"

"No, it will attract bugs," Hera said and snapped her fingers. "Should be all clean."

"You cannot tell that it was filled with refuse two seconds ago," Augustine said cheerfully. "Would you like to walk along the water, the sand, or the boardwalk?"

"Water, please," Hera said shyly. "Thank you."

"For what?"

"For being so relaxed and understanding about the food mishap. For walking with me in the water, even though you clearly don't want to get your feet wet. For not running away screaming after everything went wrong on this date." Hera rolled her eyes, frustrated with herself.

"Not everything has gone wrong," Augustine said.

"Really? What hasn't?" Hera asked, hoping for a silver lining *somewhere*.

"I got to hold your hand for a long walk. We felt warm sunshine on our faces. I got to see you in a beautiful dress." Augustine kissed the back of her hand. "And we still have the rest of the day together."

"Wow." Hera couldn't stop the heat creeping over her cheeks and knew her cheeks would appear a rosy red. "You're right, that does all sound pretty great. Thank you."

"My pleasure," Augustine replied, eyes twinkling.

# CHAPTER SIX

AUGUSTINE HAD TO force himself to focus. He was being tossed around as if he weighed no more than a rag doll.

He *definitely* weighed more than a rag doll. He was fighting a bear shifter today. Mind you, *fighting* was a bit of a stretch.

Augustine rolled to his feet and shook out his shoulders. He was *supposed* to be winning today. Instead, he kept finding himself scouring the stands for the mysterious woman in purple or thinking about Hera.

In his mind, the two women had blended together. He wasn't sure why. Hera didn't wear dark makeup and he'd barely caught a glimpse of the woman in purple. But there his brain went, mixing them together anyway.

He caught a nasty left hook in his right hand, making the crowd cheer loudly.

*Maybe my brain put them together because they have similar curves?*

Augustine twisted the other man's arm behind his back, bringing him to his knees. He pressed down heavily, and the other fell to the sand.

*I need to stop thinking about Hera's body.*

At the beach, Hera had said the sun

was too hot to continue wearing her dress. She had snapped her fingers and stretched out on the blanket in a lilac one-piece that did nothing to hide her curves. Augustine had to admit that it was a tasteful swimsuit, but nonetheless, he had to rein in his self-control tightly.

*Maybe my brain decided that lilac and violet are practically the same color?*

The bear shifter twisted his legs around, hooking Augustine behind the knee and throwing him off-balance. The two men rolled in the sand, each fighting for control over the other.

Augustine could feel the wall near his feet and pushed off, the strength in his legs giving him the extra momentum to flip on top of the bear shifter. Augustine pinned the man down and the whistle blew.

The two men got to their feet.

"The winner of this match is Augustine McKellen!" the referee announced, raising Augustine's arm.

Augustine smiled and waved robotically at the audience, as was expected of him, and left for his ready-room as soon as he could.

He sent off a quick text to his brothers letting them know he'd won and spent much too long crafting another to send to Hera. She still didn't know about his job at the fight club.

*What would she think?*

He had to tell her soon. Perhaps, this weekend when he brought her to the stables. And then there was the little matter of his own supernatural status...

Finally, he sent her a text saying he

was thinking about her and got in the shower to get the sand and grime off his skin.

*I did say I was thinking of her.*

He looked down his body at his half-hard cock. Hera in her frilly little yellow dress on the weekend popped into his mind's eye again, the skirt swishing around her thighs. She'd looked incredible astride the bike, the muscles in her calf accentuating their slender curve.

*I want to kiss every inch of her.*

Augustine soaped up his body, avoiding the place he so desired to touch. He needed to get all the dirt off before he could have his fun. The hot water cascaded over his shoulders, warming his muscles nicely, and he watched the grey water swirl down the drain until it turned clear.

He sucked in a deep breath, and the imaginary Hera changed into the lilac swimsuit. Augustine braced himself on the wall of the shower. His free hand rubbed across his chest from one nipple to the other and then arrowed down between his legs, the back of his hand bumping the crown of cock at his belly button. A breath hissed out between his teeth.

*I am already so sensitive!*

He closed his eyes, visualizing Hera's body, the way she'd filled out her bathing suit, the tight material straining over her expansive bosom, the slight darkness and peaking where her nipples were...

Augustine gasped as his cock throbbed, weeping slightly, untouched as of yet.

*Will she like sweet, gentle sex?*

He curled his fist around his shaft, giving it a light squeeze.

*Something rougher?*

His hand moved faster at the thought of Hera stretched out beneath him, moaning his name as he pounded into her.

"Oh Goddess," he groaned, bending forward as he fought to keep his wings from exploding into existence in the tiny shower stall.

The smug expression on Hera's face after she'd won their dart competition was what did him in, though, shooting his release against the wall as he bit down on the forearm that was supporting his weight. He worked himself through the aftershocks, little spurts dribbling out to wash immediately down the drain with the water.

When he was too sensitive to touch any longer, he rested both forearms against the wall, his head between them, and tried to catch his breath. His tail curled around one leg and Augustine wondered when that had appeared.

Finally, after cleaning the wall, he turned off the water and got out. He dried himself off quickly and got rid of his tail before rubbing the lotion into his skin. He was mostly purple instead of his pale human skin tone, and scales were evident on his abdomen.

Augustine had just pulled on his shirt when there was a knock on his door. He opened it hesitantly. Last time someone had knocked, it had been a proposition.

*What if the lady who sent it decided to come down here herself?*

But it wasn't a lady. It was Odin, the owner of the fight club.

"Is everything All right, sir?" Augustine asked, proud of himself for his voice remaining steady.

"That's what I wanted to ask you. You don't usually let yourself get beat up that much," Odin asked, peering intently into Augustine's eyes.

Augustine let out a short laugh. "Let? I am not sure what you're talking about, sir."

"Harumph," Odin snorted. "If that's how you McKellen boys want to play it, that's fine. People pay good money to come watch you fight, and you always put on a good show, so I have no complaints. You just seemed off today. None of your normal patter.”

“Sorry, sir. I was a little distracted.”

Odin barked a laugh. “Did that lass bed you good last week? You thinking about her?”

Augustine frowned in confusion. “Bed me? What lass?”

“Didn’t get her name?” Odin slapped the doorframe with his hand as he chuckled. “Fortunately for you, I know who she is. Sort of. She didn’t give me her name.”

The dots finally connected in Augustine’s tired brain. “The woman in purple who was sitting next to you last week? She sent me the letter?”

“Sure, boy! When a woman goes after what she wants, she gets it.” Odin winked at him. “Well, if that’s all.” He moved to leave.

"Wait!" Augustine grabbed Odin's shoulder. "Who was she? Tell me everything you know about her."

Odin paused to look down to where Augustine's hand gripped his shoulder. He appeared to come to some internal decision to allow the contact, and then raised his grey-blue eyes. "Not much. She's a friend of Chloe's, though. You could try asking her." When Augustine didn't answer, Odin continued, "Lucifer's wife Chloe?"

Augustine let go of the man's shoulder in dismay. "Thanks."

"Not a problem. See you in a few days." With that, Odin left down the long stone tunnel that lead back to the arena.

Augustine sighed, picked up his duffle, and tucked his cell phone in his pocket.

*I am not sure why I would want to find this woman. I want to get to know Hera better, not some mystery woman who saw me fighting and wanted me to fuck her.*

Resolving to put the woman in purple out of his mind, Augustine headed for home. He was seeing Hera in four days, and he wanted to make sure that the date went well. Not because hers had some rather disastrous failures, but because he wanted her to enjoy herself.

*Although, now that I think about it, maybe I should not plan the* perfect *date. I do not want her to feel worse about last week.*

He had decided to take her to the stables that were in Purgatory rather than search for one topside.

Who knew how mortal horses would react to bearing a dragon shifter?

All animals seemed to have some sort of sixth sense when it came to supernatural beings. Augustine had seen enough animals shy away from him that he didn't want to give Hera any reason to be nervous around him.

***

"Oh my goodness, these horses are gorgeous!" Hera gasped excitedly, taking in the large black mares that pranced in their stalls.

"Night-mares," Augustine corrected her. "They are used to supernatural riders, so we should not have any problems with them."

"That's so smart," Hera said, taking his hand and beaming up at him.

"Come, I will introduce you to the owner." Augustine led her over to the man in charge. "Hera, this is Diomedes." To the large man, he added, "This is her first time riding."

Diomedes grinned and uncrossed his meaty forearms. "I'll pick out a nice, gentle mare for you. You should walk her around the paddock a couple of times to get used to her before you take her out."

"I'll take that under advisement," Hera said seriously.

The three of them entered the large stable that was filled with horses. Augustine took a deep breath in, smelling the mares' sweat with an undertone of manure. It was a comforting scent, one that hadn't changed, even after all the years he'd been asleep.

"Dream shouldn't give you any trouble, Miss Hera," Diomedes said, stopping in front of a stall with a mare that looked like all the rest. Dream bobbed her head, one large brown eye moving from Diomedes to Hera.

"Ohhhh, she's beautiful," Hera murmured.

"You can pet her nose," Dicmedes suggested.

Cautiously, Hera raised one hand and brushed it over the mare, who held still during her petting. "She's perfect."

Diomedes chuckled. "She's plenty docile. Not much spooks her."

"Might I ride Fantasy again?" Augustine asked, looking across the barn to his usual horse.

"Go right ahead," Diomedes said,

waving a hand in dismissal.

Augustine, confident in Hera's ability to bond with Dream, left her to it and reacquainted himself with Fantasy. "Hello, pretty girl," he crooned as he approached her. "Remember me?"

She bobbed her head in the semblance of a nod and nudged his shoulder with her nose.

"Want to go for a ride with someone really special to me? She is going to be riding your friend Dream. Does that sound like fun?"

Fantasy fixed him with one of her large eyes and softly nickered.

"That a girl," Augustine said, opening the door so she could walk out. He grabbed her bridle and slipped it over her nose. He took up the reins and walked her back over to Hera. "Ready to go for a walk?"

Hera was astride her horse, Diomedes having helped her ready her horse and climb up onto the mare's back. "I have to admit, I wasn't expecting my first time on a horse to be bareback."

"The night-mares refuse a saddle," Diomedes said. He shrugged. "At least they're willing to put on a bridle, otherwise we'd have quite the time riding them!"

Augustine hopped up and swung a long leg over the horse, settling himself confidently on her back.

"Damn," Hera whispered.

"Sorry?" Augustine asked. He'd heard her, of course, but he liked the positive attention.

Hera cleared her throat and blushed lightly. "I said, 'damn,' because watching you was incredibly hot."

Augustine smiled shyly at her, glad she felt confident enough to say that out loud. "I am sorry I missed your mount."

"Oh Goddess, I'm not!" Hera laughed. "It wasn't flattering at all!"

"I will be the judge of that," Augustine said playfully, almost shocked at his audacity.

Diomedes, who they had forgotten about, coughed loudly, drawing their attention. "Sorry to interrupt your flirting, but a few things to remember, Miss Hera. Grip with your knees—"

Augustine tuned the rest of his lesson out and watched how Hera moved with Dream. She was already sitting taller and more comfortably. He smiled to himself, pleased with how well she was taking to riding a horse.

"I'm ready to try walking around the field, now," Hera said to Augustine.

"It is called a paddock," Augustine told her. "Let us go." He followed her out of the stable, instinctively ducking his head when they passed the large door, even though it was more than tall enough for him, even astride his horse.

They walked the horses beside each other alongside the fence.

"How do you feel?" Augustine asked.

"A little bit jolted around," Hera said. "You don't look like you're bouncing all over the place. How do you do it?"

Augustine glanced sideways at her and winced. Her breasts were jumping with each movement; it looked painful. "I grip with my knees and try to rise and fall with the horse. It is less likely to hurt your pelvis as well."

Hera shifted slightly, trying to take his advice. "I think that's better," she said. "I'm not sure I could handle anything faster than a walk, though."

"That is all right. I quite like walking with you," Augustine said. "Are you ready to try leaving the paddock?"

"Yes, let's go!"

They rode together for a while in silence, enjoying the scenery. Eventually, Augustine broke it. "I have a question."

"Go for it," Hera responded.

"Demi caters for events, correct?"

"She does, yes. I look after the shop when she does events, if they happen during the day. In the evening, sometimes I go with her." Hera glanced at him quickly. "Why, do you have an event you'd like catered?"

"Oh, no, nothing like that," Augustine

said quickly. "No, I had heard that she catered for events topside?"

"Yes, that's how she and Charles got to know each other better," Hera said. "Oh, I get it. You're wondering how she got the food across."

"Yes." Augustine was relieved she'd figured out his question.

"She doesn't. She rents a kitchen topside and does all the cooking there. It's a bit more work, but obviously worth it." Hera chuckled. "Can you imagine bringing that mess into an upscale event?"

"That would be quite traumatic," Augustine agreed. "Watch out!"

Dream stumbled in a burrow, throwing Hera from her back. Finding herself riderless, Dream tossed her head, and ignoring Augustine's calls, took off back the way they had come.

Augustine immediately scrambled from Fantasy's back, gripped the reins securely and rushed to Hera's side. "Are you all right?" he asked, worried. "Is anything broken?"

"I'm fine, I think," Hera gasped. "A bit winded. Is Dream okay?"

"She took off for home, so I doubt she hurt herself," Augustine said, giving Hera a hand up. "And her reins are short enough that even if they slip, she is unlikely to trip herself."

"I hadn't even considered that!" Hera cried. "I'm glad she's not hurt. How far back is it?"

"Quite a ways, unfortunately." Augustine indicated Fantasy. "We can ride double. Come on." He gently lifted her onto the horse and then climbed on behind her.

"This is cozy," Hera said, leaning back against his chest. She tipped her head up to look at him. "I think I like riding horses like this."

Augustine clucked to the mare, who started walking back. "I do too," he murmured, and pressed a kiss to the top of her head.

# CHAPTER SEVEN

"AND THEN THE murders began!" Chloe said dramatically.

"Really," Hera replied, unfazed as she brought tea out from the kitchen of her apartment and started distributing it around the table. "At your job, in a book, or late-night gingerbread men snack craving?"

"Can't it be all of the above?" Chloe replied, grinning so wolfishly that Hera had to double check that her friend hadn't started shifting into her white wolf form in her dining room.

"Oh, thank you, Hera," Heidi, Chloe's best friend said. She took her cup and inhaled the rich aroma. "Caffeinated, right?"

"For you, yes." Hera raised an eyebrow at Chloe's pout. "Sorry, sweetie. You won't even be able to tell the difference, I promise."

"It's not like it's coffee. Decaf is nasty." Heidi shuddered.

"You haven't had Demi's decaf, then," Hera said, pulling out her own chair and sitting down. She pulled her pad of paper and pen closer and took a sip of tea. "Are you ready to start?"

"Definitely not!" Chloe said, leaning forward eagerly. "I want to hear all about the guy you brought home from Valhalla's!"

"What's that?" Heidi asked, cocking her head to the side the way her black wolf shifter form would.

"It's an underground fight club," Hera told her. To Chloe she added, "And I didn't bring anyone home that night." She flushed. "The one man I wanted turned me down and I was sent home licking my wounds."

"I find that incredibly hard to believe," Heidi said disbelievingly. "Look at you!"

"Thank you," Hera replied with a chuckle. She reached over to the buffet and picked up the crumpled note she had written, passing it to the girls. "But he didn't look at me. I wrote him a note, because he was one of the fighters and I wasn't allowed in the rooms without an invitation. He replied quite firmly, 'Not interested, thank you.'"

"Well, there's your problem," Chloe said after reading it. "He didn't see you first. You hadn't already established that connection. So, what's your plan?"

"I don't have a plan." Hera shrugged. "Water under the bridge."

"No way!" Heidi said, crumbs from the oatmeal chocolate cookie she'd been eating falling from her lips.

Chloe narrowed her eyes suspiciously. "All right, spill. Who is it?"

"Who is what?" Hera replied innocently.

"Demi told me you went to speed dating a couple weeks ago, the night after the fight club. You met someone, didn't you?" Chloe bounced in her seat and then put a hand on her belly with a wince.

"Did you really?" Heidi asked. "How was it? I met my husband there, too, you know."

Hera's eyes widened. "Those ladies really do have quite a good track record, don't they?"

"*Spill!*" the women half-shouted.

Chuckling, Hera held out her hands. "All right! We've been on a couple dates, and I think it's going well. He's really sweet and gentle, despite his size."

"Supe?" Chloe asked, leaning her chin on her hand.

"Shifter, I think." Hera frowned. "He hasn't come right out and told me, even though he knows I'm a Goddess."

Heidi snorted. "Sorry. Kinda hard to hide that."

"Well, yes." Hera shook her head

ruefully. "Not when my damned wings popped out during our speed date."

The other two laughed uproariously at that.

"It wasn't *that* funny," Hera pouted. "Ruined my dress. Thank Goddess for Aphrodite."

"It's hilarious and you know it," Chloe said, gasping for breath. "Ow, I need to pee. No bladder control." She left the room after heaving herself up from her chair with only a tiny bit of difficulty.

"Oh, I needed that," Heidi said, wiping tears of laughter from her eyes. "I feel like I haven't had an adult conversation in months, unless it's about the babies."

"How are they doing, if you don't mind my asking?" Hera wasn't sure how she felt about infants, but Heidi's twins were pretty cute.

*I wonder if Augustine wants kids?*

She pushed the unexpected thought away with a slight shake of her head.

"Romulus has finally mastered crawling, but Ronan hasn't quite figured out how to coordinate his legs yet, so he ends up going backward." Heidi laughed. "I've had to rescue him from underneath every piece of furniture in our living room this week alone!"

"Isn't that rather soon for babies?" Hera asked, surprised.

Heidi wavered her hand. "Ehh, not really. They're just over six months old, you know. And wolf shifters crawl early, so I've been told. Canines, and all that."

"Ah," Hera said in understanding.

Chloe waddled back into the room. "You haven't been telling any juicy tidbits without me, have you? What's he like in bed? Is he a good kisser? What's his name?"

"His name is Augustine," Hera said. She bit her lip. "And we've been taking it slow."

Chloe's jaw dropped. "Ex-cuuuse me?" She stuck a finger in her ear and twisted it. "I think my ears were blocked. I could have sworn that I heard you say you're *taking it slow*?"

"That is what I said, yes." Hera rolled her eyes at her friend. "He's old-fashioned in a lot of ways, one of them being around the topic of sex. He kissed my hand and the top of my head. His lips are very soft..." She trailed off, staring into the distance. "He gives me goosebumps every time he brushes against me," she whispered, more to herself than to the other two sitting at her table.

"Sounds like you've already caught the love bug," Heidi said, interrupting Hera's thoughts.

"Maybe I have," Hera replied softly. "Would that be so bad?"

"Only if he's on the same page," Chloe said, frowning. "I don't want you to get hurt."

"I won't. Aphrodite and Eve wouldn't let that happen." Hera clapped her hands together and picked up her pen again. "Shall we get started?"

"One last thing," Chloe said, putting a hand over Hera's. "If he *does* hurt you in any way, I'm here for you, okay?"

Hera smiled at her. "Thank you. I'm really not worried."

"Okay."

"You want this to be in a couple weeks, right? What do you have in mind for the theme?" Hera asked, and wrote quickly as the two women started talking over each other, bubbling with ideas and concepts.

***

They were going topside again for their date that week.

Hera rubbed her hands over her hips, hoping that she wasn't sweating too much. On Chloe's suggestion, they were trying out a nearby paintball arena. Chloe had said that it was popular amongst her co-workers.

Hera had forgotten that Chloe worked as a detective and most of her colleagues were cops.

Now, facing the other people who

were waiting to be let into the arena, she couldn't help but be aware of it.

She adjusted her coveralls—white, shapeless things that were covering her cute turquoise and black tank top and leggings—and rolled her shoulders under the used-to-be-heavy pack filled with paint balls. The instant she'd put it on, she had spared a bit of power to lighten her load.

But she couldn't do anything about the serious-faced warriors in camouflage fatigues that were huddling in two groups on the far side of the entry.

"Do not worry about them," Augustine whispered to her.

She looked up at him. "How can you be so calm?"

"They will not bother you. You are not wearing their colors." He nodded at them again. "They are here for their own game. There is no sport in ganging up on a new player."

"You sure?"

Augustine chuckled quietly, making her shiver at the low rumble. "Quite sure. Now, *that* group you need to worry about." He gestured past the soldiers to the others in the white coveralls given by the paintball organizers.

"Why?" Hera was enjoying listening to his explanations. He'd clearly done this activity before.

"They are here as individual players, or as a large group intending to make more friends. They will target anyone in white because they do not really know each other." Augustine tucked a loose curl behind her ear. "See how they are not conversing? They are clearly a new group of friends that do not know how to talk to each other yet."

"You are an excellent people-watching partner," Hera said playfully. "And what about you? Do I have to worry about you?"

Augustine grinned. "Most definitely. You are *mine*."

Hera shivered at his possessive tone. "You'd better watch out for me, too. Once I've got you in my sights, you're done for."

"Your challenge has been heard, milady," he replied gravely. "And it will be answered."

The whistle blew and the attendants opened the gates. "Five minutes until the whistle blows again and you may start," they told the group at intervals as they flowed through into the arena.

# HERA

Hera and Augustine separated, each trying to find a defensible position to start out from.

The arena was basically a large field, half in the forest, half on grassy plains. There were various shelters scattered at intervals, ranging from hay bales, to pallets leaning against each other, to an old car with no doors, and everything in between.

Hera knew that there was absolutely no way she could run as fast as the soldiers that had already disappeared amongst the trees. She found a spot in a corner of two pallets and, after a bit of a struggle to get the angle right, managed to release the clip that held her gun to the tank.

A whistle blew, sharp and long, carried on the wind that rustled her hair, whipping the strands in front of her face.

Hera grinned, excitement running through her. She pulled the goggles down over her eyes and peeked around the corner of one pallet. Quite a few people had already started running from one hideaway to another. She raised her gun and sighted along it, pulling the trigger multiple times and hitting a person with each paintball.

*This is fun!*

She giggled, feeling giddy. She ducked back behind her pallet and looked out the other side for more targets, shooting several more people.

When she turned back to the other side, she saw that a number of people in white coveralls were pointing in her direction and waving at their friends.

*Oops.*

*I guess I should have moved!*

She resisted the urge to use her power to teleport herself to another location—that would be cheating, after all—and peeked out again. The others were a lot closer, now.

*Yikes.*

Counting out her options was futile. She could run and possibly get hit, or she could stay put and definitely bear the brunt of multiple hits until they got bored.

*Run it is.*

Looking through the slats of the pallets, she could see that the group on the right was a little closer and there was a car on the left that looked closer than the hay bales on the right.

Hera took a deep breath and readied

herself to run to the left, and then a thought occurred to her.

*If I shoot at the people on the right, they might think I'm going to run that way.*

She jumped out to the right, taking a chance, and shot a stream of paintballs at the four humans that were creeping up on her hiding place. They dropped to the ground and, in the confusion, she whipped back around the pallets and started running to the left, the tank thumping lightly against her back with each step.

Every second that passed, she expected to feel little balls of paint splatter against her back, but she never did. She dove behind the car and pressed herself against one of the wheel wells, chest heaving as she fought to catch her breath. She glanced out behind her, expecting to see the group on the left sneaking up on her again and wondered if she'd be able to run again so soon.

The group was still there, looking in confusion from the pallet where she had been hiding to the group on the right, as if they hadn't seen her dash across the empty space at all.

She shrugged and crawled over to the left side of the car, keeping herself low. On this side, she could see some more pallet hiding places and had just made up her mind to run to those when the car rocked violently on its base.

Hera glanced up anxiously and watched as a big man with blond hair swung himself through the open front part of the car, landing beside her. He shot her a grin and her heart thumped unsteadily. "You found me quickly," she whispered.

"I watched you take out those four people and thought you might need a little help getting past the five on the other side."

"You knew I was going to run the opposite way?"

Augustine chuckled. "I made an educated guess."

"Very smart."

"I like to think so."

"So, you shot at the others to distract them from me when I ran?"

"Yes, I did."

"Sounds like I owe you," Hera said coyly.

"You do. Cover me while I go on to those pallets you were considering,"

Augustine said, nodding in the direction Hera was planning on running.

"You were followed?"

"Undoubtedly. I am a little hard to miss."

Augustine leveled her another one of his brilliant grins that made her knees go weak.

"Yes, of course," Hera managed to say without squeaking. She cleared her throat and adjusted her paintball gun. "Whenever you're ready."

He ducked into a crouch. "Now!"

Hera rose up on her knees and sighted several white-coveralled targets looking in their direction. She shot two before the rest realized that they were being targeted and they all dropped to the ground.

Augustine had reached the pallet by

this point. He held up a hand to her, indicating she should wait. She dropped back down below the front of the car and peeked out from underneath at the people that she had made duck for cover.

When they realized they were no longer being shot at, they got to their feet again and started arguing about which direction they should go.

Hera stifled her giggles, not wanting them to know where she was hiding, and looked up at Augustine, waiting for him to give her the signal to run.

He held up five fingers, counting down.

Hera nodded in understanding.

He held them up again and then readied to shoot from behind his pallet.

Hera counted to five in her head and

then she started running at the same time as Augustine shot into the group that was hunting them, hitting several before they fell to the ground again.

Hera made it behind the pallet and Augustine crowded against her, his chest touching hers after each deep breath she took. "We make a good team," she said breathlessly.

"I prefer being on your team than fighting against you," Augustine said quietly.

"Me, too."

Was it her imagination, or was he getting closer to her?

"Augustine?"

"Yes?" he murmured, his breath tickling her lips.

"You'd better kiss me right now or I won't be held responsible for my actions.”

Augustine chuckled and cupped her jaw with one hand, tipping her head up. “It would be my pleasure, my Goddess.”

The first touch of their lips was soft, a gentle, feather-light brush of lips that had her desperate for more. Augustine growled deep in his chest and ripped off his goggles, Hera pushing hers up into her hair, and then they were kissing, really kissing. He tasted like blackberry jam, some sort of tea, and a unique flavor that was all Augustine, and Hera couldn't get enough of it. His tongue stroked against hers and her knees wobbled. He caught her with his big hands on her waist, pressing her against one of the pallets and sliding one thick thigh between her legs, not separating their mouths even for a second.

Hera was just about to start grinding on his leg when the pack on her back dug into her lower back in an uncomfortable way, reminding her of where exactly they were.

Reluctantly, she pulled away, and Augustine started nipping and kissing along her jawline. "Darling... Dearest... Augustine!" she gasped. "We're in the middle of a war zone."

Augustine hummed against her throat, the deep sound reverberating in her skull. Slowly, he pulled away and nodded slightly. "You are quite right. Apologies, I got carried away." He bent to pick up his goggles, which had fallen to the ground.

"Don't you *dare* apologize for kissing me like that!" Hera said fiercely. "Next time, we'll have to make sure we've got some more privacy, because I desperately want to do that more, and at more leisure!"

Augustine gave her a shy grin. "I liked it, too."

Hera pulled her goggles back down onto her face and picked up her dangling gun. She gave him a light peck on the lips and then peered out between the slats of the pallet. "They're sneaking up on us. What's our play?"

"We fight." Augustine returned her grin. "On your signal."

"Now!"

# CHAPTER EIGHT

THE SKY WAS becoming dark, nightfall setting in when Augustine arrived at Hera's apartment above ButterNut Bakery. He adjusted his cuffs, checked his black shirt was tucked in, and fixed the knot of his purple tie. Everything ordered to his satisfaction, he rang the doorbell.

"Hello!" Hera said breathlessly, opening the door and dashing away.

"Sorry, I can't leave the kitchen right now or the sauce will burn!"

Augustine stepped into the most spacious apartment he'd ever seen, certainly larger than the bakery downstairs should have above it. Some power had gone into its design, although that much was obvious simply based on the amount of greenery growing throughout the main living space. "Your home is beautiful," he said, making his way into the kitchen. "This is for you." He handed her a candy bouquet.

"Oh, this is brilliant!" Hera said enthusiastically. She plucked one candied rose petal off and bit into it. "Delicious." She offered the other half of the petal to Augustine.

He took it gently between his lips, his tongue tracing along her thumb. Her pupils dilated slightly and a soft gasp escaped her lips. "Delectable, but it does not hold a candle to your taste."

"Oh," she breathed, a blush stealing across her cheeks.

"I could spend hours devouring every inch of you," Augustine murmured. He pressed a kiss to each fingertip and in the palm of her hand.

"You..." Hera took a shuddering breath. "You must be very hungry."

"I am starving." He grinned. "How can I help with dinner?"

Hera blinked, obviously not thinking along the same lines as he was, and noticed that her sauce was boiling. "Oh no!" She immediately started stirring vigorously and the sauce settled. "You can help by setting the table. It's on the roof. The stairs are in the corner."

Augustine brought everything she indicated up to the rooftop terrace and set up the table and chairs he found there. At last, everything was ready.

Hera told him to wait for her on the roof while she got dressed. "I didn't want to spill something on my dress while I was cooking. I won't take long, I promise."

Augustine poured the deep red wine in the two glasses and picked one up, cradling it in his hand as he gazed out over Purgatory, lit up in reds and pinks simulating a setting sun.

"It's beautiful, isn't it?" Hera's voice came from behind him.

"Stunning," Augustine agreed. He turned to greet her and almost choked on his tongue. Hera had chosen to wear an almost sheer purple gown that floated around her body like the Goddess she was. She was barefoot, but he hardly noticed that, his gaze flicking from her breasts to lower. It was clear she wasn't wearing anything underneath the dress, although it was still tasteful; hinting at what he could have if only he gave the word. "I did not realize that stargazing involved making them jealous."

She cocked her head to one side, confusion written across her face.

"I doubt I will be able to take my eyes off of you to look at the stars, therefore they will be jealous of you," Augustine clarified. He blushed. "I apologize, I was trying to pay you a compliment, but I suddenly found that this wine went straight to my head."

Hera chuckled softly. "It was a beautiful compliment. Sorry, I didn't understand right away. Shall we eat?"

*Can I eat you?* Augustine thought, but did not ask. He pulled out her chair for her and then sat across from her. Each bite was exquisite. "Is this what they mean when they say that the food of the Gods is beyond compare?"

"This is ordinary cooking," Hera said, obviously pleased by the compliment. "Ambrosia and nectar are, to be strictly honest with you, overdone."

"I'll take your word for it," Augustine chuckled. "Maybe don't overcook them?"

Hera gaped for a moment, and then burst into giggles. "That's not what I meant and you know it!"

"If you say so," Augustine grinned, feeling her tiny foot nudge his leg.

They finished their meal amidst more banter, and the simulated sun had finally set below the horizon, leaving a dark sky speckled with diamonds in its wake.

"How do you recommend we stargaze?" he asked.

Hera smirked mischievously. "Stand back."

Augustine's neck prickled as he felt Hera's power assert itself. The dinner fixings vanishing, the table and chairs swishing to the side of the roof, and a soft nest of pillows and blankets appeared in the center.

"How's that?" she said proudly, hands on her hips.

"Looks cozy," Augustine said, swallowing hard. She was seducing him. He knew it. She knew he knew it. To be perfectly honest, he wanted to give in to his urges and take her, but the heavy truth of his secrets pulled him back. He sat awkwardly on the edge of the nest and took off his shoes before scooting into the middle.

"Why don't you make yourself more comfortable?" Hera asked, situating herself beside him. Her fingers delicately traced his tie up to the knot at the base of his throat. Her eyes met his, a question behind them.

"You can undo it," he whispered, his voice hoarse.

She gave him a brilliant smile and deftly slipped the fabric out of its knot until it hung flat on either side of his chest. "Buttons, too?"

"A couple," he said, and held his breath as the tight collar loosened.

"You don't have to look quite so terrified," Hera teased him. "We don't have to do anything you're not comfortable with." She pressed a kiss under his jaw and another below his ear.

"Can you kiss me?" Augustine murmured, the back of his hand tracing along her bare arm.

She smiled. "I thought I was doing that?" Her lips tracked across his cheekbone to the corner of his lips.

He turned his head slightly, catching her lips with his and drawing her into a deep kiss. He groaned, Hera echoing him. He felt her fingers in his hair, prickles of pleasure singing along his scalp, and then her weight was in his lap.

"This okay?" she asked breathlessly, tilting his head back by her grip on his hair.

"Yes," he managed to say, and then

her mouth was on his again, soft lips and softer tongue dancing with his, a sensory contrast to her tight grip on his hair.

His head was spinning.

This felt so good, so right.

He smoothed his hands down along her sides, feeling the silky material of her dress under his fingertips. When he got to the furthest point he could reach, he retraced his path in the opposite direction, the material coming with him slightly. On the next downstroke, he felt soft, bare skin under the pads of his fingers. The temptation was overwhelming. Her skin was right there. His fingers trembled...

Her hips rocked and suddenly he was aware of exactly how hard he was underneath his pants. He gasped and broke the kiss, lifting his hands away from her bare hips. "Hera," he croaked.

"Yes, August?"

"I need to tell you something."

"Now?"

"Yes. I work... I work at this club—"

Hera smirked. "A strip club?"

"What? No, an underground fight club." Augustine watched her face carefully in the dim light of the flickering candles. She looked confused, surprised, and then thoughtful.

"Valhalla's Throne?" she asked cautiously.

Augustine was surprised to hear the name falling so easily from her lips. "Yes."

"That's not a problem for me, you know," Hera said. "It's not like it's exactly unknown. I heard about it from

Chloe, Lucifer's wife."

"Of course," Augustine muttered. "It is the only place that my brothers and I could get work because they do not ask questions there. They do not ask for references, or—"

Hera cut him off again. "I don't care about your past, only your future. With me."

Augustine could only stare at her.

*That sounds so perfect.*

*Too perfect.*

"I am not ready to have sex, yet. I do not trust myself around you," he heard himself say, feeling as though he were watching from somewhere else.

Hera pulled back as if he'd slapped her. She rearranged her features into a smile a moment later, but he could still see the hurt behind her eyes.

"I am sorry." He took her head in his huge hands and brought their foreheads together. "Please understand, it is difficult for me to open up to people. I am working on it. Sex is... I..."

Hera nodded slightly. "Thank you for your honesty. I don't want you to feel pressured. We'll go at your pace." She moved off his lap and stretched out beside him. "Do you know any of the constellations?"

"I know a lot. What is your favorite?"

Hera seemed to be considering his question seriously. "I think my favorite is the Big Dipper."

"Really?" Augustine was surprised. "Why?"

"It's easy to find and you can find so many other constellations from it. Look, there it is." She raised one arm. "If you draw a line from the far end of the spout, you find the Little Dipper's North Star. And if you trace the handle, you arc to Arcturus and speed on to Spica." Her arm gestured to each of the stars in turn. What's your favorite?"

"I am a big fan of Draco," Augustine said, heart thumping harder than it had any reason to.

"Draco? It's so hard to find!" Hera protested.

"Not if you know where to look." Augustine mimicked her, raising his arm. "You find your precious Big Dipper, and Draco is right there, in between the two Dippers, curling around the little one as if protecting it."

Hera gave him an appraising look. "Most people would say that Draco is attacking the Little Dipper. Why do you say 'protecting?'"

Augustine shrugged. "People see what they want to see. Most of the stories about the stars were made up long ago. And people are afraid of what they do not understand. What do *you* see?"

"I see…" Hera scanned the sky for a long time. So long that Augustine thought she'd forgotten his question. "I see that Draco's mouth is facing away from the Little Dipper. I think he *is* protecting."

"I am glad you think so."

They spent the next few hours talking about different constellations and their histories, until Augustine surprised himself by yawning. Hera followed suit.

"I am sorry, I should leave and let you sleep," Augustine said, pulling himself out of the nest with great reluctance. He put on his shoes again and led the way down the stairs.

Augustine turned to face her while she was on the bottom step, bringing them eye-to-eye. "It is not something you did or could have done, you know that, right?"

"I know."

Crossing the dining room to the front door, a familiar piece of paper caught his eye on the buffet. "What is that?" he asked, scooping it up before Hera had a chance to see what he was talking about.

Power surged around him and suddenly, he was no longer holding the paper, but not before he saw the beautifully stylized H at the bottom.

Shock coursed through his body and he stared at Hera. "I have seen that before," he said slowly.

"Yes," she admitted.

"You knew I worked at Valhalla's?"

"Only after you brought it up tonight," Hera rushed to reassure him. "I had no idea it was you until tonight."

Augustine's brain whirled as he parsed through this new information. "You propositioned me, the next night we matched up at speed dating, and you had no idea that I was the same person?"

"I had no idea, I swear," Hera said, hands held out in apology. "I was feeling lonely that night and looking for some fun."

"How do I know that you are not still just trying to get me into your bed?" Augustine growled, gesturing at her dress.

Hera scowled at him. "I agreed to speed dating because I was tired of trying to find a hookup and I wanted something more meaningful." She stepped forward, putting a hand over his heart. "I have gotten to know you this past month. I swear to you, this," she gestured between them, "is so much more than just sexual attraction for me. I am falling in love with you, August."

Augustine let out the breath he was holding, and the anger he was feeling went with it. He cupped her face in his hand. "I feel the same."

# CHAPTER NINE

HERA WANTED TO scream.

She wanted to dance.

But most of all, she wanted to fuck.

She and Augustine had just worked through their first argument, admitted to falling for each other, and then he had left.

She looked sexy, dammit!

*Maybe I will scream—in frustration!*

The material of the gauzy dress slid

over her skin, taunting her, as she strutted back to her room. She stood in front of the long mirror—an ostentatious gilt monstrosity that had been a gift from Demi so long ago that she'd forgotten when—in the corner of her room and examined her reflection.

Her nipples were a couple shades darker than her skin tone, and peaked, begging to be played with. She could almost feel the phantom hands of her lover against her sides, brushing the fullness of her breasts as he caressed her skin. The skin at her hips burned where Augustine had touched with no barrier.

Hera whimpered, biting her lip, as she remembered the feeling of his thickness pressing against her intimately.

*I can't go to sleep like this!*

She flung open her drawers, looking for the aids she used when she wasn't interested in dealing with a man. Finally, she found what she was looking for; a suction cup dildo that she could ride hard and feel it for days afterward.

She stuck it to the floor and grabbed a finger vibrator and lube. It would take her a while to work up to being able to take the obscene cock. She ground against it, satisfied that it felt almost as thick as what she had felt growing against her when she'd been kissing Augustine tonight.

Hera's skirts pooled around her as she straddled the floor, and she reached behind her neck to release the clasp that held up the straps of her dress. The top fell to her waist, baring her breasts to the warm air of the apartment and her restless fingers. She caressed herself, feeling the weight of the globes in her palms before plucking and twisting at the nipples until they were hard and pink.

She tested her ability to take the dildo with her fingers, adding lube as a precaution.

*Not long now.*

With the vibrator, she traced her lower lips, sending her nerves into overdrive. Finding the nub of her clit, she rubbed around it, avoiding direct contact until she was gasping and begging. Finally, she touched the swollen bud with the tip of the vibrator and was off like a shot, clenching down on nothing, body shaking apart as her wings tore through into reality.

She sagged forward, hardly sated, and adjusted her hips to align with the thick cock. It took several thrusts before she fit it inside herself snugly, sinking down to the base.

"Oh *fuck,* yes," Hera gasped into the silent apartment. She put a hand over her lower belly, feeling the head of the cock pressing back against the slight pressure of her fingers. "Yes," she murmured again. Putting both hands on the floor in front of her, she raised her hips and slammed them back down again. "*Fuck* me, yes!" she cried, her wings helping drive her downward. She repeated her actions again and again until all her nerves were singing and all it took to push her over the edge was a judicious stroke on her clit with a sharp fingernail.

She came back to herself slowly, pushing up from the crumpled ball on the floor that she had collapsed into after her heightened state of arousal had washed away. The ever-hard phallus shifted within her as she moved and she gasped, oversensitive now that she had come. Lifting herself off of it was difficult, as her muscles had turned to jelly, but she managed it before collapsing on the floor once more.

"Well, that's just embarrassing," she muttered to herself, examining the sticky mess she'd made. A whoosh of power, and it was all cleared away, the ache between her legs the only lasting proof of what had happened.

***

"Isn't there anything I can do to help?"

Hera asked Demi as her sister rushed from the oven to the decorating table.

"Can you mix the green icing?" Demi asked, blowing a strand of hair out of her face as she bent over the cupcakes. "I'm going to need it next."

Hera picked up the bowl of white icing with a spoon sticking up inside it and added green food coloring. "These cupcakes are going to be based on the caterpillar from *The Very Hungry Caterpillar*, but why do you need *this* much green icing?"

"*Green Eggs and Ham*," Demi said absentmindedly as she outlined an eye on the head of the caterpillar. "That's what the cookies are for. I have the white icing already laid out, I just need the green yolk."

"Oh." Hera glanced at the cookies in

question. "I thought those were moons."

"No, I'm using the tarts as moons, each with a different phase."

"Of course you are," Hera said with a chuckle. "And what did you just put in the oven?"

"The honeycombs. Once you're done getting that icing stirred together, can you start scooping out the melons?" Demi switched icing bags, moving on to the next color. "I've already carved the watermelon, you just need to empty it and then refill it."

Hera frowned down at her bowl of green icing. "Is this good?" She showed it to Demi.

"Perfect, thank you."

Hera switched tasks, picking up the melon baller. "This is so cute! The watermelon looks like an old fashioned baby carriage!"

"That's the idea!" Demi smiled at her. "I'll carve the part I removed and re-add it as the handle, and with pineapple rounds for wheels, it'll be perfect, don't you think? Try to make the three colors of melon evenly spaced out within it."

"I'll scoop the watermelon first and put the balls on a plate and then replace them with the cantaloupe and honeydew," Hera assured her sister. She went to work, the tiny melon baller slowly eating away the pink flesh. "What else is left?"

"The main cake needs to be assembled," Demi said, nodding her head toward multiple cakes that were cooling on trays. "And the rest of the Goldilocks platter, although that shouldn't be too difficult."

"The rest?" Hera asked, curious.

"I've got the 'just right' set out already, the toppings, but the 'too cold' and 'too hot' will be last minute additions." Demi didn't look up from her decorating. "It'll require some power, naturally, to keep them at the appropriate temperatures."

"Naturally," Hera echoed. "Is the ice cream already made?"

"It's in the freezer. And the heated sauces are in the fridge, I simply have to warm them up again before we go." Demi put down the green icing pipette and blew her hair out of her eyes again. "I've got caramel, fudge, strawberry, peach, and apple," she enumerated on her fingers.

"Sounds divine," Hera said with a wink.

"Speaking of divine," Demi said, heading for the oven. "I still can't believe you didn't recognize Augustine from the fight club."

"How does that relate?" Hera demanded.

"It doesn't. I needed to change the subject." Demi chuckled. "Why didn't you recognize him? You stared at him enough, didn't you?"

"I was inside Odin's box," Hera said. "And to be perfectly honest, I wasn't particularly looking at his *face*, if you know what I mean."

"Naughty girl," Demi teased, passing by with the honeycombs. She peered into the watermelon. "Looks like you're just about done with that."

"I was thinking that, too." Hera switched the melon baller to a knife and cut open the cantaloupe and honeydew that were waiting to be excavated. Rather than deal with scooping out the seeds, she cleared them with a snap of her fingers. "What?" she asked Demi.

"Nothing," Demi replied with a smirk. "So? Have you spent some time not looking at Augustine's face in person, yet?"

"No, not yet, and it's been over a month!" Hera caught herself from whining. "I even wore the purple gown."

Demi's eyes grew wide. "In public?"

"No, at home. A night of dinner and stargazing." Hera sighed happily as she reminisced about the previous weekend. "It was really quite romantic."

"But you still want more."

"Of course I do!" Hera practically exploded. "You haven't seen him, but good Goddess, he's quite literally drool-worthy! And from what I've felt, he's—"

"Please don't finish that sentence if you're going to say what I think you're going to say," Demi said with a groan.

"Why not?" Hera asked, raising an eyebrow. "I heard quite a lot of details from you about Charles."

"Yes, because you *wanted* to hear those details. I am quite satisfied with a quick 'he treats me well and is great in bed' thank you very much."

"He does treat me well," Hera said.

"Good. You'll find the other out in due time," Demi reassured Hera. "Now get to scooping!"

"Right."

***

"This cake is *genius*, Demi!" one of

Chloe's friends gushed. "However did you come up with the idea?"

"That would be Heidi's idea, actually," Hera put in. "When we were discussing themes, I mentioned the children's book theme, and she said, 'What, like make the toilet from the cover of *Love You Forever* into a cake?'" Hera chuckled. "She probably didn't mean it literally, but I think it looks amazing, thanks to Demi's artistry."

"You helped," Demi said, not looking up from arranging the cupcakes into caterpillars.

"I held the pieces," Hera said in a stage whisper. "Why don't you each take a letter page and color it in? Chloe will turn all the pages into an alphabet book for the baby."

"What a great idea!" the woman

cooed. "I want the first letter of my name!"

"I want a W, for wolf!" another said.

"D for demon," yet another said enthusiastically.

Hera watched the twenty-four women around the silent room as they focused on their work, sometimes adding their own embellishments on the paper around the letter. "Don't forget to sign it!"

"I love this idea," Chloe said, sneaking up behind Hera and startling her. "It gives the girls something to do when they arrive and keeps them quiet for a little bit."

"You're talking as if they're a kindergarten class," Hera replied, amused.

Chloe shrugged. "If the shoe fits."

"I can hear you," Heidi said from across the room. "And I'm more like a toddler."

The others in the room laughed.

"Please finish up your letters. In five minutes, we'll be starting the games," Hera announced to the room.

"Ooh, what games are we playing?" Chloe asked excitedly.

"You'll find out with the rest," Hera said mysteriously. "If you'll excuse me, I have some things to get ready."

She left the mother-to-be with her friends and dug through one of the boxes behind the dessert table in the large conference room where the baby shower was being held. She pulled out a package of straws and a brand new baby pacifier.

Chloe was collecting the alphabet

pages from her friends, exclaiming happily over each one. Hera smiled to herself, glad that the little coloring activity had been such a hit, and started passing out the straws to the women with empty hands.

"This game is simple," Hera said, drawing everyone's attention. She held up the pacifier by the ring. "You pass this from one person to the next *without* using your hands, only the straw in your mouths. If it falls to the ground, it restarts, without the two women who dropped it."

While the guests were busy passing the pacifier around the room, amid many giggles and shouts of encouragement, Hera returned to Demi and collected the blank papers for the next game.

Once the pacifier had made the round of the room, a cheer rose up from all the women, even the ones who had to drop out. They had discovered the trick of pressing cheek to cheek and slipping the straw through the same side fairly quickly, Hera was impressed to see.

"Now that all that adrenaline is coursing through you, it's time to put those brains to work," Hera greeted them, handing half the stack of papers to the women on either side of her and gesturing that they should hand them out. "Hang onto these papers, as you'll be using them throughout the party for different games. Everyone have one? Good. Please write the alphabet down one side of the page." Hera paused while everyone bent over their papers. After they were done, she continued, "You have two minutes to write down one children's book title for each letter of the alphabet. Your time starts... Now!"

Silence reigned again as the women all hurried to complete the task and Hera smirked at Demi, who brought her the gift bag with the prize for the person with the most correct guesses.

"They seem to be appreciating the games," Demi whispered.

"Thankfully," Hera murmured back.

"What's next?"

"Open a dozen or so presents," Hera replied. "And then the memory game."

"I'll get the tray ready." Demi disappeared again.

"Thirty seconds!" Hera called out, and a couple groans echoed around the room. She grinned mischievously. "Ten seconds!" No sound met this declaration.

"Time, pens down."

After the dessert table was almost picked clean, all the presents were opened, and the last of the guests were saying goodbye, Heidi found Hera cleaning up the decorations.

"Thank you so much for organizing all of this," Heidi said, giving Hera a tight squeeze. "I had such a blast. I wish I could have attended my own baby shower." She chuckled.

Hera smiled. "I heard about that. I'm sorry. At least you got to have a party afterward."

"I did." Heidi bent to scoop up some fallen streamers. "I think my favorite game was the modification on the pin the tail on the donkey."

"You mean 'stick the pacifier in the baby's mouth?'" Hera asked with a chuckle. "I'm glad that was a hit."

"My favorite was the list of baby names," Chloe said, joining their conversation. "I know there were only twelve letters given out so that there were doubles, but even amongst just those, I got over a hundred new names to consider."

Heidi shook her head. "That would just confuse me more. We made a short list of our favorite names and then waited until we saw the boys before we named them."

"Oh, we have a short list for our little princess," Chloe said calmly. "But I want to make sure that we don't hear the perfect name *after* we've named her, you know?"

"That would be frustrating," Hera said.

"Don't worry," Heidi said. "Once your baby is named, it will be the most perfect name for her."

Chloe's eyes misted with tears. "Thank you."

"Don't start that again," Hera said quickly, materializing a handkerchief and handing it over. "Deep breaths. You're going to have an amazing pregnancy, smooth delivery, and end up with the most perfect baby girl Purgatory has ever seen."

# CHAPTER TEN

AUGUSTINE STAGGERED A bit on arrival at the winery. Despite Hera's warning about the abruptness of teleportation travel, he hadn't quite been expecting the lightning-fast whipping that had transpired as Hera moved them from outside the Underworld café to where he stood now.

He braced himself on the stone wall with one hand. "Do you get used to the after effects?" he asked, feeling queasy.

"Eventually." Hera passed him a tiny bottle. "I thought you might need this. Bottoms up."

Trusting her implicitly, Augustine took the bottle with a shaky hand and swallowed the translucent blue liquid inside. He instantly felt better. "Thank you," he said, straightening up. He adjusted his cuffs after returning the bottle to her.

"Not a problem." Hera took his offered arm and they walked around the building to the front doors.

"This stonework is beautiful," Augustine commented, admiring the winery building.

"It was modeled after a European castle," Hera replied. "I've wanted to come here since it was built, just to see the differences."

"You have been to Europe?" Augustine asked, leading her up the entry steps.

"Many times," Hera replied absentmindedly. "Mostly for work. Look at this foyer!"

The entryway was easily three stories tall with an enormous chandelier of black metal hanging in the center. The walls were built of large stones that made Augustine feel small, not an easy feat, and were covered with luxurious wall tapestries.

Augustine walked over to the nearest one, as if it would make it easier to see. "This is Greece," he said at last. "Mount Olympus in the background, one of the larger temples in the middle, and an olive orchard in the front." He stared at it a bit longer and then said softly, "It has been a long time."

Hera squeezed his hand. "I only left Greece a few years ago. It's vastly different now in a lot of ways, but not at all in others."

"Oh?" Augustine asked, curious.

"More ruins, now," she said with a chuckle. "And much less color. Time and weather wore all the beautiful statues down to the base marble. Kinda sad, really."

"That would be sad," Augustine agreed. "The statues were so vibrant. I have not been to Greece for so long. I do not think I could count the years." *Hundreds,* he thought, but did not say it aloud. Now was not the time to surprise Hera with his history.

"We'll have to go," Hera suggested,

pulling slightly on his arm to lead him to the person greeting people. "It's barely a hop from some exits back home."

"To be perfectly honest, I had not considered that potential," Augustine admitted. "I tend not to leave home very often."

"We've come here several times on dates now," Hera said, eyebrows rising in alarm. "You haven't been uncomfortable, I hope?"

Augustine smiled at her. "I have had you with me. I may have been nervous, but only because I did not want to... How do my brothers phrase it? Mess things up with you."

"Do you know, we've been dating for over a month, now, and I still haven't met your brothers. How is it that they know slang terms but you don't?" Hera asked.

"They watch more television," Augustine said. "Would you like to meet them? I have not met your sister, either."

"I definitely would like to meet them. How haven't you met Demi, yet?" Hera gasped. "For Olympus's sake, she works below my apartment!"

"I know," Augustine said sheepishly. "I have been nervous about meeting her without you being present."

"Well, we will have to remedy that." Hera nodded her head sharply.

"If you're ready to start?" the greeter said pointedly.

Augustine looked around the empty foyer, startled. "Sorry. Yes, we are ready."

"Welcome to The Gardens of Dionysus. As you can see, we have a

Greek theme to our winery, from the design of the fortress to the decor. That will carry on to our pairings that you will be tasting tonight."

"Sounds delicious!" Hera exclaimed excitedly. "I'm looking forward to it."

"Right this way," they gestured through the door behind them.

The room was exactly what Augustine expected for a wine tasting; giant barrels along one side of the room in racks, tall tables separated for the semblance of privacy, and one table at the front of the room. The walls were a continuation of the stonework in the foyer, the floor a pristine polished marble. The ceiling was lower, giving the room a more intimate feel.

There was one table left empty and they took their seats just as the sommelier started speaking to them. "Your first pairing is a—"

Augustine immediately tuned out the nasally voice of the man as he droned on about the year, color, and tones of the wine. According to him, it paired exceptionally well with olives. Obediently, Augustine took the glass that a server offered him and held it up to the light, admiring the deep ruby hue of the liquid within, and then smelled the wine, but they had been given a plate with two pungent olives and he couldn't pick out the aromas that the sommelier was describing. Augustine glanced at Hera, who was frowning into her wine glass. "It will not bite," he whispered to her.

She jumped and looked up at him. She giggled quietly. "I know that. It's just… The way he talks about wine! I can't see what he's talking about at all!"

"Me neither." Augustine heaved a sigh of relief. "I guess we are not high-society enough." He gestured around the room at the other couples, who were nodding along with the sommelier as he talked about floral tastes. "Bottoms up, as they say."

Hera gasped quietly, pretending to be shocked. "But you must taste every grape that was plucked from the vine!"

Augustine chuckled and lifted his glass to hers. They clinked them together and took sips. He picked up an olive, about to pop it into his mouth when he got an idea. He offered the small green fruit to Hera instead, holding it against her bottom lip. "Open up," he ordered, his voice husky.

She took the olive between her lips, her tongue grazing his thumb. Her bright eyes never left his, as if gauging his reaction to her flirtation.

He smiled and brushed the thumb across her lips, making her shudder and her pupils expand. Her mouth opened slightly, her breath warming his fingers.

Augustine barely registered his free hand coming up to cup the back of her head as he ducked down to press his lips to hers, unable to resist the pull of attraction between them. She kissed him back just as fervently, her mouth welcoming his tongue as it danced with hers.

He drew back, dizzy with desire, when someone cleared their throat behind them. It was another server with a new wine.

The server took away their glasses from the first round and gave them new wine and two pieces of cheese.

"I think I see why the olive and wine pairs so well," Augustine said, surprised by how raspy his voice came out. "The taste is exquisite in your mouth."

Hera giggled. "I'm not sure that's how you're supposed to do a tasting."

"If you are not sure, maybe we should try it again." He was surprised by his boldness. She brought something out in him...

Something he really liked.

"This is kefalotyri cheese," the sommelier said. "It is one of Greece's most prominent cheeses, made with goat or sheep's milk. You'll find it hard and salty, and it pairs well with this sweeter wine thanks to the lack of tannins—"

Augustine and Hera took sips of their wine and Hera picked up one slice of cheese, breaking it in half. She held one half out for him and he leaned in to take it. She moved her hand away slowly, letting him chase the food until she put it between her lips.

He smirked and tipped her head back. "You are so tantalizing," he said before claiming her. The cheese was very salty, mixing with the sweet wine and sweeter taste of Hera in his mouth.

They managed to control themselves this time, pulling away before too long. Augustine admired the blush on Hera's cheeks and the starry look in her eyes. "I could almost like wine after this, if this is the way to taste it."

Her dreamy expression evaporated, replaced by shock. "You don't like wine?

Why did you agree to this date?"

"It is with you," he said, brushing a thumb over her cheekbone. "And the painting part sounded like a lot of fun. It is just that wine is so dreadfully dull. It all tastes the same. I know that I could have told you if I was not interested in something. You would have listened and not made fun of me."

"Well, I might have teased you a little," Hera replied playfully. "But you're right, it does all taste the same."

Augustine booped her nose. "I am glad you agree with me. I would not have minded the teasing so much coming from you."

The last round came out then; a fish course.

"This wine pairs well with the Mediterranean fish—"

"Much harder to feed each other this," Augustine said of the flaky fish that was before them.

Hera picked up a fork. "You're not trying hard enough," she said, spearing a bite and offering it to him.

They ate their way through the perfectly cooked fish, sipping from their glasses as they ate, completely ignoring the sommelier's words.

"I hope the sommelier isn't the painting instructor," Hera whispered to Augustine, making him choke on the last of his wine.

He swallowed his mouthful quickly, rubbing down his sternum to ease the liquid's passage. "Warn me next time you make a joke and I am drinking, will you?"

"What joke?" Hera asked innocently.

Augustine linked their fingers together. "You are adorable."

Hera beamed at him.

"Have a good rest of your night, my friends. I bid you adieu," the sommelier said with a little bow before he left the front of the room.

"If you would follow me?" the greeter called to them from the doorway. Immediately, chairs scraped across the floor as people got to their feet.

"Shall we?" Augustine said, offering Hera his arm.

She took it and lightly stepped down from her chair.

"The painting portion of your evening will take place on the parapet of the fortress for the best views," the greeter continued.

"Views?" Hera asked. "I thought paint

nights were recreations of a painting?"

"Most are," the greeter confirmed. "We do that on days with inclement weather. But this evening is shaping up to have excellent views of the simulated sunset over the River Phlegethon."

Augustine's eyes widened. "I am not sure I could capture such beauty in paint on canvas."

Hera smiled up at him. "That's what the teacher's for. Don't give up before you even start."

Taking a deep breath, Augustine followed the rest of the group up to the highest tower's flat roof, taking in the spread of the vineyards around the fortress. Just beyond them was the vast stretch of the River Phlegethon. "Stunning," he murmured. "Limitless. Makes you want to take off and fly into the horizon."

"Very poetic," said a tall, willowy woman with oversized glasses. "Let's hope you can paint as well as you can speak." She gestured to the easels, all of which were facing the water. "Everything is set up for you, so please take your seats. My name is Phoebe and I will be your instructor for tonight."

Hera pulled Augustine to two easels at one end and picked up her brush, wiggling a little on her stool as she eagerly waited for instructions.

Augustine couldn't resist the surge of love he could feel welling up inside him.

*She is so perfect.*

*So enthusiastic.*

*A joy to be around.*

*I need to tell her.*

*I have already fallen in love with her.*

*To go another week without telling her about my dragon would be torture.*

He opened his mouth to get her attention when Phoebe began to speak. He sat back, determined to be patient and not spoil Hera's fun.

*I can tell her afterward.*

"We're going to start by sketching out the basic shapes of the scenery," Phoebe said. "You will need your pencil for this, not paint."

Picking up his pencil, he watched Hera pout as she changed her tool. "You'll get to use them both," he whispered encouragement.

She stuck her tongue out at him and he chuckled.

"Start with the horizon line. You want to make that just above halfway up your page." Phoebe demonstrated on her canvas. "Next the shoreline. Give yourself some space to work with both the water and the land."

Augustine tried to put his lines where the instructor told them and was moderately impressed by his success.

"Now, we're going to sketch out the foliage. Just make roundish shapes. Don't make them perfect or symmetrical. They're only there to give you an idea of where to put your color."

Beside him, Hera was bent so close to her canvas that her nose almost touched the fabric. Augustine nudged her ankle with his foot. "It does not have to be perfect," he reminded her. "Have fun with it."

"Right." Hera blew out a long breath. "I'm not very good at this. I think I'm nervous about not being perfect in front of you."

"Why?" Augustine asked, surprised. "I would rather know the real you than some fabricated perfect image of you. The one that brings rotten food on a picnic, that falls off her mare, that sends a complete stranger an invitation to her bed…" He winked and took one of her hands in his and stroked the soft skin on the back. "The woman who I am falling in love with is perfect for *me*, not perfection."

Hera smiled at him. "You're perfect for me, too." She leaned closer to him and added in a whisper, "Although you're pretty close to perfection."

Augustine scoffed. "I am not. I—"

Phoebe started talking again, reminding him that they were not alone. "Remember, you're sketching, not painting the next *Mona Lisa.* Now, we can start to work with color. We're going to start with the darkest darks and the lightest lights. Use a dark brown and just give the foliage a nice thin coat right at the edge. Then, on the opposite side of that, give it some white. We're drawing a sunset, so you can really lean into the shadows, but don't forget that the last light of day will be making it all glow on the other side."

The group followed the guidance of the instructor as the simulated sun set, illuminating the landscape with brilliant red, pinks, and oranges. At the end, each of them had completed paintings that, in Augustine's opinion, looked incredible.

"What are you going to do with your painting?" Hera asked him as they walked hand-in-hand back down the stairs to the foyer.

"Hang it in my room," Augustine replied. "I am very proud of myself. What about you?"

"I think I'll ask Demi if I can put it on the wall of the bakery," Hera replied. "I think it would look nice above the coffee station."

"That would—" He was cut off by a shrill ringtone.

"Oh, I'm sorry." Hera frowned as she pulled her phone out of her pocket. "I put that on 'Do not disturb,' so only emergency calls would get through… Oh!" Her expression cleared as she read the screen. "Chloe's baby is coming! I have to hurry. I'm sorry to cut our date short—"

"We have to go, now." Augustine

quickened his pace and held the front door for her. "Chloe needs you."

# CHAPTER ELEVEN

HERA GAVE AUGUSTINE a quick kiss at her door and ran inside, changing her clothes with a snap of her fingers into something more comfortable for being up all night. She grabbed a bag off a hook and started filling it with little bottles. Then she remembered she hadn't replied to the text.

*Hang in there! I'm on my way.*

One last look around her lab to make

sure she hadn't forgotten anything and then, she teleported to the front step of Chloe and Lucifer's home in Purgatory. Hera rang the doorbell. The deep chime that echoed through the house was answered by the deep barks of Lucifer's dog, Fenriz.

The heavy footfalls of the hellhound thundered toward the front door, making Hera glad that there was a solid barrier between it and her.

"*Down*, Fenriz!" a commanding voice called, and the dog's barks stopped immediately.

The door opened, revealing Lucifer, looking harried. "You're here!" He pulled her inside, closing the door behind her. "Don't mind him. He's keyed up because of all the excitement. Chloe's in the living room."

Hera followed him into the room to see Chloe curled up on the couch with a book.

"How are you feeling?" Hera asked cautiously.

"Oh, I'm fine right now. The last contraction stopped—" She checked her phone screen. "—two minutes ago. I have another three or so minutes before the next one. At least, based on previous timings."

"That's great," Hera said. She put her bag down on the coffee table. "How intense are the contractions?"

"If I'm too engrossed in my book, I miss them," Chloe said with a smirk. She raised her gaze to her husband, who scowled. "It's kinda funny."

"No, it isn't," Lucifer growled, more like the wolf shifter his wife was.

"Let's go over your birth plan," Hera said, getting down to business. "I want to remind you that whatever we agree to here will go out the window if your or the baby's health is in danger."

"Yes, I understand that," Chloe said, putting a piece of paper in her book. "I'm rather fond of the idea of a water birth."

"Not a problem. Most hospitals in the L.A. area are equipped with water birth tubs in their delivery rooms," Hera said.

"What about at home?" Chloe asked.

Hera raised her eyebrows and glanced quickly up at Lucifer's thunderous expression. "That is an option of course..." she said hesitantly.

"Great!" Chloe sucked in a sharp breath and grabbed her phone, tapping a button. "Contraction. That one was more intense," she explained. To Lucifer, she asked, "Can you please whip up a birthing tub for me?"

Lucifer sighed and threaded his fingers through his hair. "I don't even know what one looks like. Are you sure you don't want to go to the hospital?"

"How about I look her over, check on the baby, and then you can make your decision knowing all the facts?" Hera interjected.

Chloe breathed out a long sigh and tapped her phone again. "That sounds good to me."

"First thing, you need to keep breathing during your contractions. I'm going to give you a pain neutralizer. You'll still feel the contraction, but it'll only be the pressure instead of that *and* pain." Hera grabbed one of her lotions.

"Thank you," Chloe said. "I would put

that last one at about a six? I guess?"

"Good. Second, I need you to change into a gown. I'm going to need to check your cervix often, and wearing pants and underwear will hinder that. If you want a water birth, you'll need something that is easy to remove once we get to that phase. Even if we do have to go to the hospital, a gown will be much easier to deal with." Hera glanced at Lucifer again. "Would you like to help Chloe get changed?"

Lucifer leapt into action, eager to have something he could do, Hera figured.

The couple vanished up the stairs, and Hera quickly spread out the things she would need, including her book for taking notes on the progression of labor. She considered calling a birth tub into existence, but left that for Lucifer. Instead, she drew a detailed diagram of one with all the things that Chloe would find useful during birth.

By the time she was finished, Chloe had returned. She dropped onto the lounge right when another contraction hit.

"Very good," Hera said. "If you don't mind lying back and spreading your knees... Perfect." She took a quick look, estimating the dilation. "You've still got a ways to go. You've lost your mucous plug. Did your water break yet?"

"Did I?" Chloe asked choppily between breaths. "I must have lost it on the toilet. I didn't notice. No water, yet, I don't think."

"Trust me, you'll know," Hera said with a chuckle. "Let's get that lotion on you." She slathered it on thickly, working it into the taut skin of Chloe's distended belly, around to the sides, and part way down her upper thighs. "Does that feel better?"

"Instant relief," Chloe said with a sigh.

"I still need you to track the feelings of pressure," Hera said. "Can you sit up? This needs to go on your lower back as well."

"It's like a mini massage," Chloe said happily. "This stuff is a lifesaver."

"I am good at what I do," Hera said absentmindedly, rubbing the lotion in. "We'll have to reapply this every two hours, and every one hour once you get in the tub. Now, let's check vitals."

Once Chloe was lying back again, Hera listened to both Chloe's and the baby's heartbeats, marking them down along with the time. She got permission from Lucifer to call a continuous monitor into existence, and hooked it up to Chloe's belly, explaining everything as she went along.

"Everything looks better than good," Hera said, getting to her feet and facing the couple. "There's plenty of time to decide, but what would you *like* to do?"

"I'd really rather be here at home where I feel safe," Chloe said pleadingly to Lucifer.

Hera almost smirked, but kept her face neutral. Chloe was pulling out the big guns.

"Show me this tub," Lucifer said with a sigh.

"She'd be very comfortable, and you could get in behind her to support her,"

Hera said, pointing to her sketch. "She can do just her labor in the tub, or the whole thing. The baby would be in no distress. Coming out in the water has been theorized to be less traumatic for the baby, according to some studies."

"Really," Lucifer drawled. He looked at Chloe, reclining on the lounge, one hand on her belly. "If this is what she wants, then this is what we will do. But the instant, and I mean millisecond, that there is any trouble, we are going immediately to the hospital."

"Of course," Chloe said serenely. "How long do you think we'll have before the big show?"

"I'll know better in about half an hour when I check you again," Hera said. "Then, I can estimate time based on progression."

"Honey, I need to pee," Chloe said suddenly, sitting up straight. "And maybe…"

Hera held out her hand, helping Chloe to her feet. "You don't have to worry about the baby coming out, yet. You can go to the bathroom with no worries."

Chloe looked at her gratefully. "Thank you."

"And you had better not be squeamish around body functions," Hera said sternly to Lucifer as Chloe left the room. "You're going to help with the diapers, right?"

Lucifer drew himself up and frowned. "Of course." He took a hesitant step after Chloe. "Should I go with her?"

"We'll keep an ear out if she needs help, but she should be fine on her own," Hera replied. "The tub, if you please?"

Lucifer squinted at the paper again and then one side of the spacious room was filled with the perfect replica of Hera's drawing, in pink.

Hera smiled. "For the baby?"

Lucifer flushed. "Too much?"

"It's perfect. Why don't you go get some towels? One tea towel, to drape over the baby once she's here, and several larger ones for drying her off."

Chloe returned just after Lucifer. "Oh!" she exclaimed when she saw the tub. "It's perfect!"

"How are you feeling?" Hera asked, helping her to sit back down.

"Fine. I had another contraction while I was on the toilet, which took some extra time because my body didn't really want to do what it was supposed to do." Chloe sounded frustrated.

"Don't worry. Your body is doing exactly what it's supposed to do." Hera checked the time. "I can check you again, if you like, or we can wait another couple minutes."

"Now, please," Chloe said. "I'm eager to know the timeline."

Hera chuckled as she checked her. "Looks like we'll be here for a while. You haven't progressed much at all. Do you have any cards?"

"Should we be worried?" Lucifer asked quickly.

"Not at all," Hera replied calmly. "The monitor would tell me immediately if there was any change that I need to be aware of. The baby's just taking her time. It'll give your body time to adjust," she said to Chloe. "This is fine."

Lucifer breathed a sigh. "I'll set up a table."

***

Several rounds of cards later, after Chloe had dropped off to sleep, Hera and Lucifer were talking quietly on the couch on the other side of the room.

"Chloe tells me you're getting serious with one of Purgatory's residents?" Lucifer asked.

"I am." Hera smiled at the mention of Augustine. "He's a shifter of some sort, although, I don't think he ever mentioned what type."

"What's the name?" Lucifer asked, frowning slightly. "I know most of the shifter families."

"Augustine McKellen," Hera said.

"Very tall, quite muscular, blond, one of three brothers. He said they arrived here fairly recently."

"McKellen," Lucifer said musingly, eyes staring off into the distance. "Hmm."

Hera got to her feet as the monitor changed its tone.

"What does that mean?" Lucifer asked, panicked. "Hospital?" He held up his fingers, ready to teleport them all.

"No, it means her body is ready to push." Hera gently woke Chloe with one hand on her shoulder. "Do you feel a strong pressure?"

Chloe blinked her eyes sleepily. "I'm not... Oh. Yes, I feel that."

"Would you like to get in the tub, or would you rather stay here?" Hera asked.

"Tub, please," Chloe said, struggling to sit up.

Hera offered her support. To Lucifer, she said, "Wait until Chloe is in, and then fill the tub to just below her bellybutton with warm water. No more than eighty-eight degrees."

Chloe unsteadily stepped into the tub in between contractions and Lucifer took her other arm to help her sit. Chloe hung on to Lucifer's hand. "I need you," she whispered.

Hera's heart ached at the mutual love practically tangible between them and turned away to fold Chloe's gown, storing it on the lounge out of the way. When she turned back, Lucifer had filled the tub with the exact amount of water Hera had requested, and was sitting behind Chloe, supporting her with his body.

"No, I need the real you," Chloe repeated. "Please."

Lucifer locked eyes with Hera's. They turned molten as he transformed from his human form into demon, red tipped black wings extending from his shoulder blades coming to encircle Chloe as well.

Hera nodded, not surprised or afraid of the demon lord's true form. "How are you feeling, now, Chloe?"

"Perfect," Chloe purred, nestling into her lover's all-encompassing embrace.

"That's what I want to hear. You've got a contraction coming up. Brace your feet on the bottom, knees up. Lucifer, hold her by her thighs. Chloe, you need to push down with your inner muscles as you draw your knees in to your belly. Like you're curling up in a ball. You're going to push down... Now!"

Chloe grunted.

"Breathe, good. And relax," Hera coached. "Again. Very good. Relax. One more... Good. You can rest in between contractions. Do you have any questions, do you need anything changed?"

Chloe lazily shook her head from side to side. "I'm good."

"You're doing great, sweetheart," Lucifer murmured.

"Here comes another contraction. Ready and... Push!"

The water sloshed in the tub as Chloe's body forced itself through the intense waves of pressure over and over again for more than an hour.

Chloe sagged back against Lucifer's chest, tears trickling down her cheeks. "I don't know if I can do this anymore," she rasped.

"You can," Hera said firmly. "The baby's crowning. She's almost here. Two more pushes. You can do this."

"You've got this, my love," Lucifer said.

"Get ready," Hera said. "Here it comes. Push *hard*!" She reached into the tub as the baby's head appeared. "Another push for the shoulders!" she said over Chloe's shout. The baby slipped easily out and Hera scooped her up, dropping her in between Chloe's breasts and rubbing the baby's back gently.

A healthy cry warbled out of the little girl's mouth and then she was quiet, eyes opening slowly.

"She's here?" Chloe said

incredulously.

"She's here," Lucifer affirmed in wonder. He stroked the back of one finger down the baby's back, sharp claw carefully away from the soft new skin. "She's perfect."

"Lucifer, do you want to cut the cord?" Hera prodded the new father from his enraptured state as he stared at his daughter.

"Oh, yes! Sorry. She's just so... "Lucifer flashed that mega-watt grin.

Hera chuckled, and then pointed to a small area on the cord where she'd placed two clamps, and handed the beast the scissors.

Lucifer fumbled with the small shears for a moment in his huge demon claws, and then managed to snag the pair of metal blades with the tips of two nails, quickly snipping the cord where Hera had indicated.

Hera quickly swiped the baby's eyes with a cloth, covered her with a warm tea towel, and checked on Chloe. "You've got a bit of a rest until the placenta arrives. Bond with the baby. I'm not going anywhere," she added when the new mother looked up at her with panic in her eyes.

A little later, Hera dealt with the rest of the delivery, checked Chloe, and then dealt with all the new baby things that had to be done while Lucifer helped Chloe to the bathroom.

"Aren't you the sweetest little bundle of joy?" Hera cooed to the tiny baby. She efficiently swaddled the baby in a light blanket and watched, heart melting, as she closed her eyes and drifted off to sleep.

Lucifer returned, in his human form, and carefully picked up the baby, tucking her against his chest. "Chloe wanted to lie down. Did you need to check on her again?"

Hera nodded. "Yes, but not until later today. The baby will wake up in a couple hours and will be hungry. Text me and do skin-to-skin with her until I get here and then I can help Chloe with the first latch. Oh, I almost forgot..." Hera handed Lucifer two labeled bottles. "The instructions are on them. One for her breasts, to promote lactation and to ease swollen nipples, the other for the vulva for the pain."

"Thank you. From Chloe, myself, and Atlanta," Lucifer said as he walked her to the door.

"Beautiful name," Hera said with a smile. "I look forward to seeing more of her. Get some rest, if you can."

Lucifer smirked. "I think you know how well that advice will work."

"Better than you think. You may not have been the one to give birth, but you're more exhausted than you realize." With that, Hera transported herself directly to her room and toppled into bed for a two-hour nap.

# CHAPTER TWELVE

"WAKE UP, SLEEPYHEAD!"

Augustine rolled over with a groan and pulled his pillow over his head. "Mmm mm, mm mmm, mm?"

"Sorry, didn't quite catch that." His sanctuary was ripped off of his head and he growled, on all fours and on top of his brother Jaden in seconds. They rolled, fighting for dominance, and knocked over an end table, the things on top of it falling to the floor with a crash.

"Take it outside," Finley ordered from the doorway. "Or better yet, stop?"

"Not until he apologizes for waking me up," Augustine said, his tail flicking his ankles in clear agitation. "What was so important?"

"It's almost noon," Jaden said and shrugged. "You're a bear to wake up on the best days, but you won't sleep tonight if you stay in bed past noon."

"Oh, I am sorry, are you my father?" Augustine growled. "Since when do you decide on my bedtime?"

"When your pacing keeps me up at night!" Jaden shouted.

"This is the first I have heard of it!" Augustine's voice rose to meet Jaden's. "I will just leave and walk the streets when I cannot sleep, if you cannot handle me walking about in my own home!"

"Now, boys," Finley tried to calm them both down.

"You shouldn't be out in the middle of the night! What if someone thinks you're up to no good?"

Augustine laughed bitterly. "I can take care of myself. Besides, I have a date tonight. I'll be out late. Do not wait for me to come home before you get your beauty sleep."

"It's Hera again, isn't it?" Finley worried at his bottom lip. "Have you told her, yet?"

"No." Augustine shook his head, calming down. His dragonish attributes melted away. "I am planning to tell her tonight."

"That's just great!" Jaden scoffed.

"And what if she decides that we're too dangerous to live? A Goddess with powers is nothing to sneeze at! Plus, she's friends with the lord's wife. Who knows what *he* may do when he finds out what we are!"

"I think you are blowing this out of proportion, brothers," Augustine said. "Hera is not like that. Even so, you cannot change my mind about tonight."

"You haven't fucked her, yet, either?" Jaden asked bluntly.

"*That* is none of your business," Augustine said coolly. "I told her about my job a couple weeks ago. She took it well."

Finley cuffed Jaden upside the head. "A job isn't the same thing as your dragon."

Jaden stuck his tongue out and

walked out into the hallway with the parting shot of, "If she's a bitch about your dragon, I'm not going to wipe your tears away, big boy."

Augustine growled deep in his chest, his tail reappearing and lashing angrily between the bed frame and the desk chair.

"He's just being an asshole," Finley told him. "Get yourself under control."

"I am under control," Augustine grumped, sitting in the desk chair after pushing his tail out of existence once more. "He does not get to insult my love—"

"You love her?" Finley asked quietly, interrupting Augustine's rant.

Augustine opened and closed his mouth a couple times. "I guess so," he said sheepishly, rubbing a hand through his hair, messing it up more than his sleep had. "I knew I was falling in love with her, but I did not…" He swallowed hard and raised his gaze imploringly to his brother. "What if she reacts poorly to my dragon?"

"Then, she's not the one for you," Finley said, shrugging. "I know that sounds callous, but you don't want to be with someone who doesn't love you completely. *All of you.*"

"Exactly. That is the reason why I have not… We have not…" Augustine sighed. "It does not feel right to progress on a physical level when I have not bared my soul to her."

Finley grinned. "So, you haven't fucked her."

Augustine growled low and Finley raised his hands in a peace offering.

"Sorry. Not your point. You feel as though your secret, that you're a dragon, is holding you back from being with Hera intimately. Once you tell her, provided she's all right with it, you'll be able to go all the way?"

"It is beyond just the secret of who I am," Augustine said, throwing his arms dramatically in the air. "I do not enter into intimacy lightly. I want the woman I make love with to be the only woman for me. She must accept my mating bite, be mine forever."

"Whoa." Finley sat on the edge of the bed. "Sorry, still reeling from the fact that you're a virgin. Do you think Hera is the one for you?"

"If she is not, I will be alone for the rest of my life. I cannot imagine any woman more perfect for me than Hera,"

Augustine said passionately.

"Whoa," Finley said again, staring at Augustine. "I don't think I've ever seen you like this. Is there anything I can do?"

"Keep Jaden off my back," Augustine said with a snort. "Hopefully, I will not need anything beyond that."

"I'll do my best. He's fighting tonight, so he's a bit on edge. You know how he gets."

"I do," Augustine confirmed. He stood. "I need to do my workout and then, get ready for my date."

"Good luck," Finley said, standing as well and closing the door behind him as he left.

*I do not need luck.*

*I need a healthy dose of courage.*

He changed into his running

clothes—loose black shorts and a royal blue muscle tank—and left by the front door. Augustine took his time to stretch, working each muscle carefully until the soreness from the previous night's fight had left them. Bouncing a little on the balls of his feet, he took a deep breath of fresh air, grateful, yet again, for the cleaning up in Purgatory that Lucifer had done once he'd met his mate, Chloe.

Waving to one of his neighbors, Augustine started off down the road, deciding on the forest path today. He'd be going topside later tonight for his date, and he didn't enjoy crossing the gate more than once a day; it made his skin crawl.

The heat from the simulated sun gave way to cool shade as he passed under the canopy of leaves. The concrete sidewalk changed to hard-packed dirt and he picked up his pace, feet thudding firmly on the well-worn path.

As he got deeper into the forest, dew-covered branches hovered low and he had to duck to avoid them. Small creatures, not unlike squirrels and chipmunks, scurried along branches and out of sight with each step he took. Rays of light filtered through in splotchy patches, illuminating wildflowers and exposed roots of trees.

Augustine took a deep breath in and let it out slowly, embracing the silence and solitude. He and his brothers had woken to an entirely different world than the one they had fallen asleep to. So many more people, so much more noise, and technological advances that felt like magic.

The witch that had put the brothers to sleep until their soulmates were both alive and ready to receive them had warned them that times would change. She made sure that they had understood this. Not wanting to live a life of solitude, the brothers had agreed to the terms and had hidden deep in the mountains, protected from the passage of time or discovery by the witch's protections.

But when the earthquake had awoken them a few years ago, they had been faced with a foreign world. Fortunately, Odin had found them wandering topside and had brought them to Purgatory, found them a home, and given them jobs while keeping them off of Lord Lucifer's radar. They owed Odin everything.

Thinking about Lucifer brought his

thoughts to the demon lord's bond with his mate, Chloe. She had accepted his claim, his bite, after knowing him for only a few short months, and, now, they were married with a baby. Augustine wished he could ask Lucifer how to go about such a sensitive conversation. But then, he'd be on Lucifer's radar—something he and his brothers had managed to avoid for the past few years and hoped to continue.

Augustine reached the large meadow in the middle of the forest and leaped forward, transforming with barely a thought into his dragon form. Purple scales rippled over his skin, large leather wings exploded from his shoulder blades, and his long tail whipped over grasses as his size grew to ten times that of its original. He made sure to keep below the tops of the trees as he glided around the circumference of the open space.

After he lost track of the number of laps, he landed on all fours next to the stream at one side, bending to drink from the cool water. The glimpse of his beast's reflection made him uncomfortable and he transformed back to human. He dunked his head, flinging water every which way as he shook his hair like a dog. Scowling down at his reflection, Augustine wondered if he'd ever feel comfortable in his skin.

*Maybe if Hera accepts me.*

As if Hera's name triggered something within him, he glanced up at the sky. The simulated sun was below the trees. Without being any closer to an idea of how to tell Hera about his dragon tonight, Augustine headed for home and a shower.

He didn't linger in the shower, not wanting the teasing from his brothers that might ensue, and got dressed in black jeans and a dark purple dress shirt that matched his scales. He styled his hair quickly, noting that it was getting a little long and he'd need to make an appointment with the barber soon. Hair that was too long was a liability in the ring—it provided an easy grip for opponents.

The walk to ButterNut Bakery was long enough for him to panic over *still* not having any idea how to broach the subject of his shifter status.

He knocked on Hera's door with his heart in his mouth, thankfully, not literally, and when she opened it, he blurted out the first words that came into his mind. "I am a shifter!" he almost shouted at her.

Hera looked taken aback at first, but then she smiled at him. "Thank you for finally trusting me enough to tell me."

Augustine digested what she said slowly, his ears ringing slightly from his high anxiety. "Wait... You *knew*?"

"You use my lotion," Hera said patiently. "I know every scent I make. You had me smell your wrist on the speed date."

"Right." Augustine felt like the floor had fallen out from underneath him. He almost sagged with relief. He offered her his arm. "Shall we?"

Hera beamed up at him and took his arm, locking her door with a snap of her fingers. "Why all the secrecy? Surely, you didn't think I would care?"

"It is not exactly common," Augustine admitted. "I did not realize that you had lotions designed specifically for my brothers and me."

Hera frowned. "But—"

Augustine didn't understand her confusion. "A lotion that covers dragon shifter characteristics must be different enough from the others that you can tell between them," he said, trying to clarify.

Hera's jaw dropped and she came to a stop in the middle of the street. "*Dragon*?" she squeaked.

"You said you knew..." Augustine replayed their conversation in his mind. "I did not say that part out loud the first time." He cursed. "I am sorry." He led her to the side, clearing the street. "Are you all right? Does this... Does this change how you feel about me?" he asked anxiously.

"I…" Hera closed her mouth tightly and gazed deeply into Augustine's eyes. At last, the tension in her body relaxed. "I don't feel differently. You are August, the man I've fallen in love with. No matter what hearsay there was about that type of shifter in the past, you are obviously not the person about whom the rumors spoke." She tucked her hand through his arm again.

"I have heard the gossip," Augustine said, a muscle in his jaw jumping. "My brothers and I were asleep long before those allegations started. I do not know the person or people spoken about in those rumors. But we are not evil."

"Definitely not," Hera agreed.

Augustine's brain finally caught up to

all Hera had said. "You love me?" he asked, hardly daring to hope.

"I do."

He wanted to shout it from the rooftops, his heart felt full to bursting. "I love you beyond all comprehension," he said, picking her up in a tight hug and twirling her around in a circle and laughing.

When he put her back on the ground, Hera smiled up at him and cupped his cheek in one tiny hand. "We're in love."

Augustine kissed her lightly. "I feel like I could fly."

"Can't you?" Hera replied impishly, laughing a little.

"I can." An idea came to him then. "Let us get dinner to go, topside, and then, I will fly us to a remote island that I am familiar with. It is not big enough for cruise ships, and too far away for most day trips by smaller boat, but I can get us there in no time."

"Nobody will see us?" Hera asked, bouncing a little in excitement. "Will I be warm enough in this?"

Augustine looked her over—now that his anxiety had disappeared, he could appreciate her appearance—she was wearing a halter dress very similar to the one she had worn to the speed dating event, but in a deep blue with silver accents. Her arms were bare. "Can you not—" he snapped his fingers "—make a coat appear for you if you get cold?"

"I could do that," Hera agreed. "How will we be unseen? It's still daylight."

Smirking, Augustine replied, "Humans do not notice me. It is only the supernaturals that I have to worry about."

# CHAPTER THIRTEEN

"HUMANS CAN BE so oblivious," Hera said with a chuckle as they walked into a nearby Chinese food place. She breathed in the tangy aromas. "Oh yes, that'll hit the spot."

Augustine chuckled. "We will get all your favorites."

"*All* of them? I don't think I can eat that much," Hera replied with a saucy grin.

"As much as you want, then," Augustine said.

They ordered several dishes to share and packed them in a backpack that Hera pulled out of thin air to appear on the floor.

Augustine winked at her as he bent to pick it up from their feet and filled it with the still steaming containers. "I hope that this is insulated."

Hera passed her hand over it. "Of course it is."

"It is, now," Augustine teased her quietly.

She nudged him in the ribs, making him chuckle again.

*I like this playful August.*

*He seems more confident and less shy.*

*His secret must have been eating him*

*up inside.*

That made her think about what he had just told her again.

*August is a dragon shifter!*

Even though there had been rumors surrounding dragon shifters for as long as Hera could remember—that they were all gone and that they had been evil—Hera couldn't bring herself to believe them. Obviously, the dragons weren't all gone. Augustine, and presumably his brothers, were proof enough of that. And if that rumor was patently false, the other had the potential to be as well.

Hera's gaze met Augustine's as he closed up the backpack.

*He is* not *evil.*

*I trust him.*

*He is a dragon, and he is my love.*

*I do not doubt what is in my heart.*

Hera took Augustine's hand and squeezed it. "Let's go."

They walked hand in hand to a secluded hilltop overlooking the beach. Augustine put down the backpack and started to pull his shirt over his head and toed off his shoes.

"Here?" Hera asked in surprise. "There are so many people around, they could look up at any second."

He slipped his pants down to his ankles and Hera felt her face flush with heat as she tried to avoid looking below his waist. He stretched one arm and then the other.

"Another thing about humanity," Augustine said, a twinkle in his eye, "they never look up, either." As he spoke, purple scales and ridges rippled over his skin, a long tail popped from his lower back, thick sharp claws replaced his hands and feet, and then his body grew and expanded, and suddenly standing before her was a large violet colored dragon.

Hera's jaw dropped. "Oh, my Goddess," she whispered, one hand rising instinctively to stroke along one pronounced eye ridge. When human, Augustine had clear blue eyes, his dragon form's eyes were a deep, dark purple, and seemed to be endless in their depths. Hera could see herself reflected in the wide pupil. "You're beautiful," she breathed.

"I need you to seat yourself above my wings," Augustine's deep voice rumbled through the air, vibrating in her chest. He offered her a bent front leg to scramble up.

Hera stuffed his clothing in a side pocket of the backpack and then tugged over her shoulders. She climbed quickly up his leg, finding it easy to mount him, and settled on his shoulders. She held onto the horns that stuck out a bit more than the rest, and squeezed her knees slightly. "Ready."

"Hang on," Augustine said, his body vibrating between her legs.

And then, they were off.

He launched forward, powerful muscles throwing them into the air, wings catching the closest updraft and forcing them up, up, up at a rate that had Hera struggling against gravity.

Eventually, they evened out, and Augustine beat his wings, gliding forward as smoothly as a boat through water. Hera recovered enough to sit up slightly, gazing around at the unbelievable view. The land was receding rapidly behind them, only the ocean visible on all sides. The sun was glaringly bright in her eyes, preventing her from seeing the island Augustine had mentioned.

They flew for a while. Augustine's warmth between her legs wasn't enough to keep the rest of her from feeling the chill in the air, so Hera called a thick shawl into existence between her skin and the backpack. Next, warm woolen mittens wrapped around her hands so that she wouldn't have to let go of Augustine.

The sun had almost set by the time Augustine dropped altitude. He changed the angle to go slightly to the south and dropped even more.

Hera peered ahead eagerly, seeing a tall, dark shape on the water. "Is that it?"

"Yes."

The landing on the beach was quite graceful, in Hera's opinion. Augustine's wings caught the air and slowed them down until his feet touched the sand.

She reluctantly slid from his back, banishing her warmer garments as the tropical heat hit her face. The instant she was on the ground, Augustine transformed back into his human form and she handed him his clothes from the bag. He hastily pulled on his clothing and then, taking her hand in his, he pulled her toward the trees.

"I want to show you something," he said, a bright smile on his face and excitement making his eyes twinkle. "We can eat there."

Hera's heart thumped giddily in her chest, following him through the tropical forest and ducking under low hanging vines until he stopped abruptly.

"Close your eyes," he said. "No peeking."

She followed his instructions, anticipation taking hold in her chest. He grasped both her hands in his, walking with her slower, now. After a few minutes, he told her, "Open them."

"Ohh!" she gasped, looking around the tropical oasis with awe. The first thing that drew her eye was a waterfall, the water dropping into a pool surrounded by palms and night-blooming flowers. Beside that was a stretch of rocky beach, with stones big enough to sit on. "August, this is beautiful! I can see why you love it here." Hera threw her arms out and spun, taking it all in. "I can't decide what I want to do first; go for a swim, eat, or examine your dragon more leisurely now that there's nobody around to interrupt us."

Augustine coughed. "How about we eat first?"

***

The Chinese food had remained the perfect temperature in the insulated backpack and they ate heartily.

Hera put her chopsticks in an empty container and got to her feet, stretching her arms over her head. She looked up at the almost full moon, which illuminated the little oasis almost as clearly as if it was day, and smirked. "I think I'm ready for a swim, now," she said coyly. "But I didn't bring a bathing suit. Whatever will I do?" She played with the tie at the back of her neck.

"You could make one—" Augustine's voice cracked. "What are you—"

Hera shimmied out of the rest of her dress, dark blue material pooling at her feet. Her underwear joined it a second later, leaving her wearing only moonlight. "I am going for a swim. You're more than welcome to join me." The way to the pool passed by Augustine's seat, and she trailed one hand over his chest and up into his thick hair as she made her way to it. "In fact, I would be very disappointed if you don't," she said over her shoulder. Encouraged by the fact that he had twisted around to keep his gaze on her, she emphasized the swing of her hips a little more than usual, and at the water's edge, she bent to test it with her fingertips.

A low groan met her ears and she smirked to herself. "The water's beautifully warm," she announced, stepping into it. It was the perfect depth; shallow with a slow drop off until the water would have been over her head at the base of the waterfall. She stayed away from the pounding water, not wanting to get caught underneath it in case of trouble, and ducked her head under to get her hair wet. She came up, smoothing her hair back, to see that Augustine had decided to join her, after all.

She swam back over to the shallows, walking up the slope to greet him, and held out her hand.

Augustine visibly swallowed, his gaze flicking from her face to her body and back.

Hera smiled. "Do you like what you see?"

"Yes," his voice was hoarse.

"So do I," Hera replied, lingering on his nicely muscled body, obliques that narrowed down to a long, thick cock. Her mouth watered and she felt wetness between her legs that had nothing to do with the water they were standing in. Finally closing the distance between them, she stood on her tiptoes and kissed his jaw.

His chest heaved against hers and he tilted his head down until she could align their lips. She pressed light kisses against his mouth until he growled deep in his chest and bent, grabbing her by the thighs and lifting her so she could wrap her legs around his hips.

"Yes," Hera murmured into his mouth, weaving her fingers through his hair so she could manipulate his head the direction she wanted. Her tongue licked into his mouth, dancing with his as she deepened the kiss. His cock rubbed against her clit just right and she broke the kiss with a gasp. "Oh, my Goddess, yes!" she cried out, grinding her hips against him.

His hands tightened their grip on her thighs and he walked deeper into the pool until the water came up to their chests. "I thought you wanted to swim?" he groaned as her hips swiveled.

"I wanted to get us both naked," Hera clarified, tipping his head back to expose his throat. "Swimming is incidental." She bit lightly over his Adam's apple, and his fingers dug into her flesh even as the water around them thrashed. "Is that your tail?" she asked, eager for another glimpse of it. "Can I see?"

"Yes," Augustine gasped.

His tail rose up out of the water beside them and Hera stared at it, eyes wide. Hooking one arm around his neck, she reached out for his tail with the other, bringing it close. "How much can you feel with it?" she asked.

"I can feel each individual finger holding it," Augustine replied.

"Is it sensitive? Can you feel the difference between a soft touch and a firm one?" Hera asked, stroking the purple scales with a fingertip. Although the edges looked sharp, they did not cut her finger.

"Yes," Augustine responded shakily.

"Can you feel the difference between the air and the water?" Hera brought the tip of his tail closer to her, brushing the tip against her cheek. The scales felt soft and warm against her skin.

"Ye-es." His breath hitched as Hera flicked the tip of his tail with her tongue, her gaze fixed on his. His pupils darkened and the irises flared indigo when she sucked more of the tail into her mouth, her tongue undulating against the thick length. "Hera," he said, a hard edge to his voice. "You are messing with things you do not understand."

Hera pulled off the tail tip with a pop. "Did that feel good?" At Augustine's nod, she smirked. "Then, I know exactly what I'm doing."

Augustine twitched his tail out of her grasp, making her pout. "Touching my dragon parts like that makes the rest of me want to go full dragon."

Hera's inner walls clenched on nothing. "That sounds amazing," she rasped. "Yes, I want that."

"You cannot possibly—" Augustine shook his head. "I have no idea what I could do to you in that state."

Hera took his chin in her hands, forcing him to see the sincerity in her eyes. "August, when will it get through to you that I love you. All of you. And I *want* you. *All of you.*" She frowned. "You do want to have sex with me, don't you? Now that you don't have any more secrets, we can have sex, right?"

Augustine sighed and released his grip on her thighs. "Follow me," he said, swimming toward the waterfall.

Confused, Hera swam under the falling water to see a cavern hidden behind it. Augustine was climbing out of the water and sitting on the rocky edge. He patted the spot beside him and she joined him.

He took her hands in his and met her gaze unwaveringly. "I have one more secret," he admitted. "It has to do with my dragon. When I mate, if we were to make love, I wish for it to be forever. I wish to give you my mating bite."

"Are you— Are you proposing?" Hera gasped, eyes wide. Her cheeks flushed. "I..."

"Yes, I guess I am." Augustine cleared his throat. "I don't have a ring." Then, an idea seemed to strike him. Pulling his tail around, he felt along it for a second until he tugged and a scale came off. "Take this, as a sign of my devotion to you."

Hera took the shimmery purple scale in a shaky hand. She cupped it between her palms and concentrated, shaping the material. When she finished, she held up a dainty purple ring. "Put it on for me?" she asked shyly.

"Does this mean—?" Augustine seemed hardly able to believe what he was seeing.

"Yes," Hera whispered. "I will be yours forever."

Augustine took the ring and slid it on the fourth finger of her left hand. "I love you," he murmured, cupping her face.

"And I love you," Hera replied, beaming at him. She slung her leg over his hips, sitting on his thighs and bringing their lips together in a passionate kiss. "We can have sex, now?" she asked eagerly, pulling back slightly.

"We could wait until after the wedding..." Augustine suggested playfully.

Hera crossed her arms under her breasts. "Don't you *dare*!"

Augustine leaned down and licked at one pert rosy nipple, making her shiver. "I could not resist you even if I wanted to. I only hope that you will be patient with me. I have not... This is new territory for me."

*And I propositioned him!*

She bit her lip. "I promise I will teach you how to bring me pleasure. Can I start with something that I love?" Hera scratched her fingernails through the shaggy hair at the base of his neck.

"Anything you love doing, I want to do," Augustine said breathlessly, his eyes half-closed.

"Good," Hera purred. She moved her hands over his shoulders to his chest, down his pecs to his thighs. "Your body is in *amazing* shape. I want to feel you all over, but first, I have been *dying* to get my mouth on you."

"Your mouth?" Augustine panted, chest heaving.

"Yes." Hera smirked at him, her lips following the same path as her hands, starting at his neck and moving down, flicking her tongue over one beaded nipple as she passed it. She slid off his lap into the water and pressed his knees apart with her hands, moving in between them until her breasts pressed against him.

"Oh..." Augustine squeaked.

"Is this all right?" Hera asked, trailing one finger along the thick raised vein on the underside of his cock. "This is one of my favorite things to do to a man and I haven't done it in a long time. You might need to move my head for me."

The noise that escaped Augustine's mouth could only be described as, "Hnng," but Hera took it as consent.

"Tell me if you want me to stop," she said and licked up the length of the vein, her saliva dripping out of her mouth with her enthusiasm. When she got to the crown, she pulled the foreskin down and traced the ridge with her tongue, taking her time to taste his musky flavor and lapping up the pulse of pre-cum that seeped out from the slit. "You taste amazing," Hera murmured, not wanting to pull her mouth away from his body long enough to speak. "I'm going to take you into my mouth, now."

"Thank you for the warning," Augustine gasped out.

Hera hummed her appreciation and sucked the head into her hungry mouth, continuing the rhythmic circular motion of her tongue. More pre-cum burst against her taste buds and she swallowed it greedily. Bracing herself against his thigh with one hand, the other lazily cupped his sac, caressing the smooth balls within it between her fingers. She bobbed her head down, his cock head hitting the back of her throat. Hera undulated her tongue as she came up and was rewarded by another spurt.

"You do not have to—" Augustine

started to say, but cut himself off with a groan when she descended again.

She relaxed her throat muscles, grateful for her lack of gag reflex and sank down until she buried her nose in the tuft of course pubic hair at the base of his cock.

Augustine's body spasmed underneath her and he shouted something that sounded like "Goddess!" He gathered up her hair, holding it with his big hands behind her head.

She moaned long and low, relishing the tug on her scalp as he twisted her hair in his tight grip. Hera bobbed her head a bit and resettled both her hands on his thighs for balance.

Fortunately, Augustine seemed to get the message, or perhaps, he remembered her request to move her head, and he started to glide her mouth slowly over his cock.

When she hummed encouragement, he picked up the pace, using her and forcing his cock deep inside her throat over and over again.

*Oh my Goddess,* Hera thought wildly, giving herself over to Augustine's pleasure.

*I'm going to come like this, without him even touching me!*

"Hera, darling, my love," Augustine panted, slowing his movements. "I want to... Can I end in your mouth? Please, please, tell me I can."

She lifted a thumb and hummed again, and he picked up his pace once more until Hera felt his balls draw up tight, his cock swell, and then he was exploding down her throat, his body tensing and his skin rippling between violet and his human-pale tone. He let go of her hair and she came up partway, *needing* to taste his release as he filled her mouth with his salty-sweet-sour cum.

She could feel it dripping out the corners of her mouth, hot streaks hitting her breasts, trickling down the mounds, and beading over her nipples.

The feather-light feeling over one of the most sensitive areas of her body was what finally set her off, her skin tingling as her nerve endings sang.

As suddenly as her orgasm hit, she felt herself being pulled backward into the water. She swallowed quickly, letting his cock slip from between her lips.

Augustine grabbed her under her arms, lifting her out of the water, and she felt a pull on the heavy weight of her wings, which must have materialized when she was at the height of passion.

"Thank you," she murmured, voice hoarse and throat raw as she cuddled into his chest.

# CHAPTER FOURTEEN

AUGUSTINE FELT LIKE his soul left his body when Hera engulfed his cock in her mouth.

*Goddess save me.*

He gathered up her hair behind her head, the better to see her face, and then almost wished he hadn't. The stretch of her mouth around his cock was obscene, the swell in her throat erotic beyond anything he could have imagined.

Hera bobbed her head, and Augustine remembered that she had asked him to guide her. Hardly daring to breathe, he slowly moved her over his length. And then she hummed, the vibrations echoing over every nerve ending and bringing him even higher.

*She obviously enjoys it...*

He moved her faster, chasing his completion while keeping an eye open for her discomfort. She stayed completely relaxed in his grip and soon, he could feel the end approaching. He gasped out something, he wasn't quite sure what, but Hera raised her thumb and he exploded.

Seconds later, Hera's beautiful white wings burst into existence and she was being pulled backward as they filled with water. He caught her gently and lifted her, freeing her from the weighty prison.

"Thank you." Her voice was raspy from his use of her throat.

Augustine felt a frisson of pleasure run up his spine. "Are you all right? Why are your wings out?"

"Oh, I tend to lose control over them in orgasm," Hera said dreamily. She ground her hips against his thigh and he could feel her slick wetness.

"You came?"

"I told you, I really enjoy giving head." Hera chuckled and lifted her mouth for a kiss.

He happily provided one, capturing her plush lips with his own. Their softness gave pleasantly under his tongue, his taste buds singing over the taste of his essence in her mouth. He pulled back a breath to ask, "Can I give you another one?"

"Hmm," Hera hummed happily, kissing him again. "I'll never say no to another kiss."

Augustine blushed. "I meant an orgasm."

"Oh!" Hera sat back. "I mean, same answer. How do you want to do this?"

"Can I pick you up?" Augustine smirked.

"Throw me around as much as you li—" Hera broke off with a squeak when Augustine slipped his arms under her thighs, lying back and lifting her over his shoulders. "Are you sure you've never done this before?" she asked breathlessly.

"I'm a fighter," Augustine said with a straight face. "I know how to manipulate a body, especially one as delicious as yours."

"You know, I don't remember the fight I saw being quite this sensual," Hera said, shifting her hips over his neck.

"That is because I was not fighting you." Augustine pulled her a tiny bit higher. Her scent was so strong at this point that he felt his cock stir again, the desire to be sheathed inside her almost overpowering. "I want to taste you. I need to feast on you. Please."

"Okay," Hera replied breathlessly.

His hands full of her ample hips, he pulled her down over his mouth and groaned at the first taste of her juices on his tongue.

*I will never be tired of her.*

He wrestled the tiny bud underneath his tongue, lashing at the swollen nub and relishing in her breathy moans.

Then, he searched farther back, finding her hot, wet slit and diving into it as far as he could go. It wasn't enough. Selectively transforming just his tongue into the long, forked muscle of his dragon, he flicked it against her walls, rubbing over and around as deep as her tight channel let him. Her cries of pleasure filled his ears and he returned to driving her ever higher by focusing on the apex of her sex.

"I need you inside me," Hera gasped.

Not ready to relinquish his treat just yet, and with his hands busy guiding her full hips, Augustine wondered what he could use to fulfill her request.

"Augustine!" Hera whined, her hands resting behind her on his chest. Her hips undulated over his mouth, directing him.

His tail thrashed in the water in time with the movement of her hips and he got an idea. She didn't seem to mind his extra appendage; she'd caressed it, even put it in her mouth. He brought it up, caressing her upper thigh gently.

Hera tensed and moaned. "Yes, yes, inside me!" she cried out, bending forward to give him room to slide in behind her.

This position mostly cut off his air supply, her hard pubic bone pressing against his nose. He didn't care, his mind focused on the sensations being provided to him by his sensitive tail as it snaked up her thigh. He spread her cheeks and used his tail to trace her creases lightly down the middle, over one divot to the next, warm and wet.

He felt the soft scales against his chin

as his tail entered her channel, the appendage getting wider further from the tip, his mouth busy with the now throbbing swollen bud.

"Oh *Goddess*, yes!" Hera groaned out, her voice muffled due to her thighs over his ears and the water pounding down beside them.

Augustine ran his fingers over every inch of skin he could reach, from her voluptuous hips to her breasts hanging just above his head. He pinched the engorged nipples and she screamed in pleasure, coating his tail in a wash of creamy honey and shaking in his grasp. He slowed the movements of his tongue, pushing it inside her to slurp up the feast she was providing for him.

Eventually, she shakily crawled backward down his body until they were face-to-face. "That was incredible," she whispered. "How did you know what I needed?"

"You are very good at letting me know what you want," Augustine said, feeling proud. "I am glad I was able to make you feel as good as you did for me." He stroked his hands down the leading edge of her wings to the bend, feeling the similarities and differences between her wings and his. Other than hers being feathered and his leather, they were remarkably comparable. "Have you ever tried flying?"

"Hmm?" Hera asked, eyes half-lidded. "Whatever you're doing feels incredible. Don't stop."

Augustine chuckled low. "I will not. Flying?" He gently threaded his fingers through her primaries, arranging them to lie flat and coaxing the water from them.

"I've never been able to control them enough for that," Hera said softly.

"Do you want to try?" Her eyes snapped open at that and he met her gaze calmly. "I would be with you every step—well, flap—of the way," he reassured her.

"What about sex?" Hera said with a pout.

"While this cave is romantic and all, I would rather be comfortable the first time we make love," Augustine said dryly.

"Oh my Goddess!" Hera gasped, sitting upright. "I forgot this was your first time! Is it okay so far? Are you having fun?"

Augustine chuckled and sat up as

well, wrapping her up in his arms and manifesting his wings to better enfold her in his embrace. "It has been amazing. *You* are amazing." He held her face gently between both hands, feeling altogether too large to touch her. "Let us go get dressed." He pretended not to notice her shivering as they re-entered the water, both their wings tucked away. "Dress warmly," he cautioned her as she started to pull on her dress.

"Right." Hera banished the remains of their meal and dressed herself in a fleece-lined jacket and pants. "What do you think?"

"Very nice." Augustine appreciated the way her new outfit hugged her curves while he pulled on his pants.

He took her hand as they walked the short way back to the beach. "Are you ready for this?"

"No," Hera said bluntly. "But I trust you."

His heart swelled at that. "I will not let you fall." He walked her through the mechanics of her wings, how to shift her muscles so that the extra appendage could flap. Once on the beach, he transformed into his dragon and had her feel his shoulder blades while he moved his wings in a slow arc.

"I think I understand how it works, but I don't know how to do it." Hera looked worried, a furrow on her brow.

Augustine booped his snout against her forehead. "I will be with you. Climb up."

Hera mounted above his wings, her warmth almost scorching. He gave his head a little shake, determined to focus and give her a pleasant and successful first flying experience. Then, he launched himself into the sky, wings beating powerfully as he climbed higher, the air whistling in his ears as he thrilled at the feeling of flying with his mate, even if she wasn't flying under her own power yet.

"Do you trust me?" he shouted over his shoulder.

"Of course!" she shouted back.

"Let go!" Without giving her time to think about it, he did a loop in midair. Hera fell off at the top, but he caught her a split second later, now flying on his back with her face down against his chest.

He nudged the top of her head, concerned that she hadn't yet raised it.

"I'm fine." Hera looked up at him.

"Just trying to get my heart to stop trying to escape my chest."

Augustine chuckled. "Bring your wings out."

"Now?" Her voice squeaked on the word.

Petting down the center of her back with one claw-tipped finger, he ordered, "Yes. Call forth your wings, Goddess Hera."

Hera gaped at him for a moment, her cheeks flushing a brilliant scarlet, before her wings made their appearance, nearly pulling her off of him as they caught the air current.

Augustine braced her, holding her against his chest. "Spread them out, angled down. Good. Now you have some control. Flap. Again. Good. Feel how the air moves under your wings. You are in control. You are the Goddess Hera. You are amazing." With each bit of encouragement, Hera grew bolder, until he relaxed his grip on her back and she rose above him, flying on her own.

She let out a whoop and wobbled, quickly righting herself.

Augustine beamed proudly. "You've come a long way already." He twitched his tail to keep himself steady as the current fluctuated.

Hera had no such appendage and dropped into his arms. "I think that's enough for tonight," she said breathlessly. She ran her fingers over his scaled chest and banished her wings, shivering. "I need you now."

"You want to teleport?" Augustine asked.

"Is that all right? You must not get

the chance to fly very often." Hera wrapped her arms around his neck and nuzzled under his chin.

"Give me a moment. There's something I've always wanted to try."

"No problem."

"Hang on." He flipped over, cradling her body in his powerful arms, and with strong beats of his wings, climbed in the air. When they were high enough, he transformed into human form and they plunged downward, twined together in an embrace. He shouted in exhilaration and then turned back into dragon form, catching the next air current that swooped them safely away from the water.

"Warning!" Hera gasped. She slapped his chest with one hand. "That was terrifying!"

"If you were that terrified, you would have teleported us," Augustine replied smugly.

"I'm going to do that, now."

In the next moment, Augustine found himself spiraling through the uniquely uncomfortable sensation of her teleport, and then they were in her living room. He instantly felt too big for the space, something that made him intensely uncomfortable.

"Hang on," Hera said, and made several gestures once he put her on her feet. "I can get you a bottle of that travel potion if you need it."

The walls, which had felt too close a moment ago, seemed much further away, now. The doorways and hall to her bedroom had increased in size. Augustine looked around the apartment, completely distracted from the gurgling of his stomach from the rough teleport. "Did you... You made your apartment bigger? For me?" His tail lashed behind him, not encountering any impediments.

"Of course." Hera ran her hand along his jaw. "I want you to feel comfortable here, in whatever form you choose."

"Goddess, I love you," Augustine breathed, changing to his human from with barely a thought and hugging her tightly to him.

"Take me to bed," Hera purred in his ear, wrapping her legs around his waist.

"With pleasure," Augustine growled, his long strides taking them quickly to her bedroom, despite it being further away than it had been a few moments prior.

He placed her gently on the foot of

her bed. He brought her left hand to his mouth, kissing over the violet ring she wore. "I do not want this evening to ever end. I cannot go back to seeing you only on the weekend."

Hera raised an eyebrow. "Isn't this ring an engagement ring? I fully expect to see you as often as possible until we move in together."

"I need you," Augustine breathed, encouraged by her words. "I need you like I need air."

"Then take me," Hera said, snapping her fingers and removing her clothing.

"Oh..." Augustine swallowed his disappointment. There would be other times.

"What's wrong?" Hera asked, obviously attuned to his mood shift. She blushed. "Am I too forward?"

"No, I..." Augustine cleared his throat. "I wanted to take your clothes off. Take my time."

"I'm sorry!" Hera gasped. "I didn't even think about that. Hang on..." She snapped her fingers again and she was wearing a pair of baggy grey sweatpants and a loose black spaghetti strap tank top. "Better? This is what I wear when I'm lounging about the apartment."

His mouth went dry. "How do you look amazing in whatever you wear?" he asked, trailing the backs of his fingers along one strap over her shoulder. It was quite obvious that she wasn't wearing a bra, and he didn't quite understand why her wearing shapeless clothing was turning him on faster than her being naked.

"You get to undress me, but I get to

undress you as well," Hera said playfully, hooking her fingers in the waistband of his jeans and pulling him snugly between her legs, rocking him back and forth. She started at the bottom of his purple dress shirt, the buttons slipping easily through their holes and slowly revealing his skin.

Once she had opened enough, she started pressing her mouth over his heated skin, peppering kisses along his chest and outward to every inch of his skin that she could reach, her fingers tracking higher and higher until she pulled the shirt off his shoulders, letting it pool behind him.

Augustine shivered in anticipation as she worked open the button and fly on his jeans and yanked them down his legs. He kicked off his shoes and stepped out of his jeans before ordering her, "Lie down. It is your turn." He took off his socks before crawling up onto the bed, hovering over her. "You are so beautiful," he whispered, his fingers catching in her curls as he stroked her cheek. He wasn't fully paying attention to her legs, which had wrapped around his hips.

Hera smirked up at him and suddenly he found himself lying on his back, her hair creating a curtain around their faces.

"That is so hot," he murmured, tracing her jawline with one finger. He kept going, down her neck to the strap of her tank top, the other hand joining in the fun on the other side. Her breasts were hanging low, the material of the top gaping and showing off her cleavage. Slowly, hardly daring to breathe at his audacity, he trailed his digits along the tops of her breasts and gently pulled the material down. "Okay?" he asked hesitantly.

"Please," Hera whimpered.

At her approval, he pulled the material the rest of the way down, freeing her breasts, cupping them in his large palms and pushing them together over the top of the tank. He ran his thumbs over her dusky nipples, watching them tighten and draw in until they became hard points. "Your body is so responsive," he said, sliding one hand around her back to rest between her shoulder blades and thrusting his hips up.

Hera was thrown forward with a little yelp, her wings popping out in her surprise.

Augustine grinned, not only did he get to touch her beautiful wings, but her breasts were now directly in his face. "Tell me what feels good," he said before drawing one beaded nipple into his mouth, tracing nonsense patterns over the hard little bud with his tongue and then, biting down softly. His fingers buried themselves in the downy fluff at the base of her wings, searching for her sensitive places.

She writhed in his grip, panting above him. "*Augustine!*" she gasped. "Too good! I'm going to come!"

Satisfaction curling deep in his belly, Augustine released her breast. "I want you to orgasm for me, I want you to end untouched. If you do, I will fuck you with my tail again until you soak your panties with your fluids. Then and only then will

I flip you over and enter you, finally joining together as one."

"*Ohhhhh fuck*, August!" Hera whined, thrusting her hips ineffectually over his abdomen.

He smirked up at her and sucked her other nipple into his mouth, biting down at the same time as he pressed his fingertips hard against her wings.

Hera arched, crying out as she shattered in his arms.

"Yes, my Goddess, you are perfect," Augustine hummed against her. His hands left her feathers to glide over her hips, pulling her sweatpants over the swell of her ass. His tail nimbly slid inside the material and stroked over her hot, wet pussy. "I cannot wait until I am inside you. You feel like heaven." In so saying, he thrust his tail into her soaked core without warning.

# CHAPTER FIFTEEN

HERA WAS BARELY coming down from her previous orgasm when she felt cool air on her ass and then her twitching pussy was filled with the tapered end of Augustine's tail. It unerringly went straight for the sensitive spot on the front wall of her channel and she already felt like she was on the edge again.

Assaulted by the trio of sensations— his hot mouth on her breasts, his fingers in her wings, and the thrusting of his tail deep inside her—it was all she could do to catch her breath. "More, give me more!" she gasped.

Augustine looked up at her, one eyebrow raised in a cocky expression that shouldn't be that attractive. Hera almost scowled at him, but then she felt his tail curling inside her, swelling until it was twice as thick. "Oh fuck, yes," she moaned. "August, I want you. I need you!"

"Remember what I said," Augustine replied, sounding amused. "I want you to make a mess of your clothes. Orgasm for me and I will gladly join with you." His tail punctuated his words with short, sharp thrusts that had her spiraling.

"Keep doing that—" Hera cut herself off with a non-verbal shout. "Yes! There, keep it—" And then she felt like she was flying again, all her nerves ricocheting with pleasure signals that were almost too much to bear.

When she recovered, she felt empty and wet, her pants sticking to her skin in an uncomfortable mess. "Oh my Goddess," she muttered, her face flaming. She covered it with one hand.

"What was that?" Augustine asked, awe coloring his tone.

"It's called squirting," Hera mumbled. "It doesn't happen all the time, just when I'm stuffed full."

"So beautiful," Augustine murmured, pulling her down his body so he could join their mouths. "You are incredible." He slid his hands inside her pants, pulling them down further while he rubbed along her thighs.

Hera lost herself in the plushness of his lips, relishing the way he took care of her. She twined her fingers through his hair, gripping at the roots and tipping his head back, both of them gasping for air. "My turn," she breathed, sitting up and bringing him with her. Continuing the arc, she laid back on the bed, wings spread out to the sides.

*One of the benefits of making the apartment bigger, is that I won't accidentally knock something over with my wings.*

Augustine slid the sweatpants down her legs, tossing them off the edge of the bed and crawled back over her, nibbling and licking his way up her body, skipping over the rolled-up tank top under her breasts.

"This mating bite you're going to give

me," Hera said, moaning slightly when he flicked his tongue over a sensitive nipple.

"Yes?" He switched sides.

"Do you have to be a full dragon when you give it?"

Augustine sat up abruptly, shocked. "No! Goddess, no! My head as a full dragon is bigger than your whole body!"

Hera giggled and reached up for him, coaxing him down to her body again. "Okay, good. Just checking."

"I'd bite clean through you," he grumbled, folding back over her.

"Can I banish this?" Hera asked, indicating her top.

"If it is uncomfortable," Augustine said. "I am afraid I cannot get it over your wings."

Hera snapped her fingers. "There's

one more article of clothing on you that needs to go," she said, hooking her toes into the waistband of his underclothing. She reached between them to lift the elastic over his cock and then used her feet to pull them the rest of the way down his legs.

Augustine's jaw dropped. "You know what you are doing."

"I'd better." Hera cupped his cheek in one hand. "My experience doesn't bother you, does it?"

"As long as my inexperience is not off-putting for you," he replied, pressing a kiss to her palm.

Hera chuckled. "Not even the tiniest bit." She hooked her legs around his hips and guided his cock toward her throbbing pussy. "I believe you promised me that we would make love? Please, I need you inside me."

"Are you sure you are prepared to take me?" Augustine's hand joined hers between them, testing her readiness.

"I am so ready that I will combust on the spot if you don't take me, now." Hera demanded forcefully.

"Tell me if it hurts," Augustine warned, and then she felt his cockhead at her entrance.

She relaxed, assured that he would take care of her, and he slid inside her slowly. "*Goddess*, yes! You feel amazing," she groaned. When he was fully seated inside her, she rocked her hips, grinding her clit on his pubic bone. "It feels like coming home," she gasped.

"So good," Augustine managed to say. "Can I move?"

"Please!" Hera whimpered. She felt

every inch of him as he pulled out and entered again, still moving at a snail's pace. "Faster, August. I'm not made of glass."

"I thought slow was the romantic way?" Augustine replied, an adorable furrow in his brow. "I thought we were making love."

Hera gripped his biceps, her fingernails digging into the skin, and caught the flare of violet fire in his blue eyes. "Making love is what two people do no matter what when they have sex. The speed doesn't determine the amount of love. I need you to go faster, please."

"As you wish, my Goddess," Augustine said, slanting his lips over hers.

*That should have been enough to warn me*

She clung to his arms as he started snapping his hips forward and back in a rapid pace that had her reaching orgasm in seconds. He slowed only to give her a little time to recover, and then quickened until she was screaming his name again.

This time, when he slowed his pace, he kissed down the side of her neck, licking the muscle over her shoulder. "I will not be able to hold off much longer. May I..." He trailed off, blushing.

"You're currently balls-deep inside me and you can't say 'come?'" Hera asked with a slightly hysterical giggle.

"May I... *come*... inside you, my love?" Augustine said, obviously unfamiliar with the word.

"Fill me up!" Hera replied enthusiastically. "I want it all."

That was the perfect thing to say, as

Augustine pounded into her with renewed energy, letting loose a low growl in her ear that made goosebumps erupt all over her body.

"Come with me, Hera," he ordered and then, he bit down on the meat of her shoulder hard when he thrust in deep one last time, sending her spiraling into ecstasy.

The pulse of his cock inside her was giving her pleasant little aftershocks, the way wavelets lapped at the shore after a bigger wave. She ran her hands down his back, feeling his sweat-covered muscles tremble under her touch.

"Is it always this intense?" Augustine murmured into her neck, collapsing down onto his forearms and trapping her.

"I have never felt this much emotion

for a lover before," Hera admitted truthfully. "I only imagine that our mating bond is what increased the passion."

"Are you teasing me?"

"Maybe a little." Hera kissed his pout. "I love you."

"I love you, too." He frowned. "I need to clean that bite. Do you have a potion for that?"

"I do, but it won't work on me." Hera winced as he pulled out of her, missing his girth already. "My potions never work on me. We'll have to clean it the mundane way."

"Bathroom?" Augustine asked, pointing to a door.

"Closet. Bathroom's in the hall." Hera admired his ass as he walked out of the room uncaring of his nudity. Her fingers trailed down her body, slipping into her stretched out pussy and coming out dripping with their combined fluids. "Mmm," she moaned, bringing her fingers to her lips.

"What are you doing?" Augustine asked, returning. "Are you still—?"

"I *crave* your touch," Hera begged. "I feel so empty without you. I need more."

"Let's take care of your shoulder first," Augustine said, walking behind her and placing a warm cloth on her skin.

"Feels so nice," Hera purred.

*Just a little wiggle and... Ah, there we go.*

She twisted her head to the side and licked a hot stripe up his ball sac to the root of his cock, tasting both herself and his cum.

"You are making this incredibly difficult," Augustine said, amusement coloring his tone.

"Hurry up. I want to ride your dragon."

Augustine's breath caught in his throat, and he coughed, pulling away. "Are you sure?"

"One million per cent," Hera said. "Though maybe it'd be best if you don't go full size." She giggled and brought both hands down between her thighs, spreading them wide to make room for her fingers. "I want to feel you so deep inside me, splitting me open until I can't walk tomorrow without feeling like you're still there."

"I do not— My dragon does not look human," Augustine hedged.

"Of course not. You're a dragon."

Then Hera caught on. She sat up and spun to face him. "Do you have a hemipenis?"

"Not exactly." Augustine looked conflicted. "There is only one, but the head is quite large, like a knot, and I will not be able to extract it for quite a while after release."

Hera quickly checked her chin in case she was drooling. "I am *very* okay with that."

The wet cloth that Augustine had been holding dropped to the floor, his tail lashed in the air. "You are the perfect woman for me," he breathed.

Hera preened. "Come on, big guy." She shifted to the side of the bed and indicated the center. "On your back."

He looked dubiously at the soft mattress. "My weight will break the bed."

"If it does, I can fix it. Lie down," she ordered. "Transform, please." Hera watched with pleasure as Augustine's skin rippled into the purple scales of his dragon as he partially transformed. The bed creaked and Hera strengthened the frame with barely a thought.

Augustine's dragon belly was a shade lighter than the scales that covered the rest of his body. She ran her fingers down the lighter scales until she got to the slit above his tail. It was already gaping a little, and she coaxed it further by rubbing tiny circles around the edge. "Come on, August. Show me your cock," she crooned, bending and licking around the opening.

Something nudged her chin and Hera raised her head to see the bulbous end of his dragon cock. "Oh wow," she breathed, watching it grow in length and girth as it rose from the slit. Her pussy throbbed with longing, wanting to get it inside her as soon as possible. "Can I touch you?" she asked.

Augustine made a growling noise deep in his chest. "Yes."

She started by wrapping her hand around the shaft; the texture was smooth and felt a lot like human skin. She wasn't sure if she'd been expecting dragon scales, but it was nice to feel something familiar.

The head was a different story. At first, Hera thought it was covered with tiny spikes, but when she ran her finger over one, they proved to be soft to the touch. She palmed the head, caressing it with both hands until Augustine rumbled something that sounded like a purr.

"If you keep touching me like that, you won't be able to fit it inside you," he warned, his voice a deep rumble that made her shiver.

Hera chuckled. "You underestimate my determination, but I'll take your word for it." She straddled the large dragon, his cock rubbing against her apex without even trying. "This is going to be so much fun," she murmured, encircling his shaft again and holding it steady. She had to rise up onto her heels to align herself properly, the spikes making the head feel almost fluffy against her nether lips. It was a strange feeling, but exciting. She rocked her hips slightly, enjoying the sensation.

Augustine clenched his front claws. "I am worried—"

"If it hurts, I'll stop," Hera said soothingly. She relaxed and pressed down, each spike adding to the usual sensations of being entered. She could feel once the head had passed through her entrance, her body enveloping it and tightening as she continued the downward motion along the shaft. "Goddess, Augustine!" she cried out as she bottomed out, throwing her head back as she gasped for breath.

"Does it hurt? Are you okay?" Augustine asked quickly, his wings flexing in agitation.

"No hurt. Feels good. So deep," Hera managed to say between heaving breaths. She put a hand over her lower abdomen, feeling it distended slightly, and pressed against him. He twitched inside her and she moaned. *"Fuck,"* she murmured, biting her lip. Gathering her strength, she rose up and lowered herself, moving slowly until she was sure she could take all of him easily. Each pass was easier than the previous, her body excited beyond anything she had ever felt before. "I'm going to let gravity take over," she told Augustine as she reached the peak of her motion.

His eyes widened, the purple iris of his dragon like fire behind the clear blue eyes of the man as he struggled to keep his size in check.

Hera relaxed her muscles, falling to the base of his cock in one swoop, her shout of pleasure harmonizing with Augustine's.

"You liked that, didn't you," she gasped. "I can feel your crown swelling inside of me."

The spikes felt like ribbing as they traveled over her inner walls, something that she always enjoyed.

*I really need to find a better name for them than that, because they're not sharp.*

She repeated the thrust-fall several more times until Augustine roared and flapped his wings. Hera found herself manipulated delicately by giant claws as he changed their positions, placing her on all fours underneath him. Hera was thrust forward into her mattress as he drilled into her, reaching depths she hadn't known existed.

Glancing to either side, she could see his claws curling into her sheets, and she felt the underside of his chest as he curled over her back. She couldn't keep her eyes open for more than that, as she quickly reached the precipice of pleasure. She'd barely come down from that peak when he thrust her into the next one. She was riding high, everything becoming a blur, when something changed. She wasn't quite sure what it was at first, given her blissful state. After a moment of concentration, and trying to ignore the tingling in her nerves, she felt it again... The head of his penis had grown more, thickened to epic proportions and stretched her more than she ever thought possible.

"I am going to fill you up," Augustine rumbled above her, his wings and body surrounding her. "Hera, I am close. I cannot hold it in any longer."

"Yes, August, yes! Fill me!" Hera cried. The rush of hot cum was heralded by his bellow. Her eyes rolled back in her head as she came yet again, squeezing him for every drop he had to offer her.

She returned to consciousness slowly, Augustine's heated body surrounding her with warmth. Hera stretched out and caressed what she could reach of his still scaly forearms. She felt full—more than full—stuffed with the large head of his cock in her extended channel, and pressed one hand over her lower belly, biting back a moan.

"Are you awake?" Augustine asked quietly. "I am sorry I was so vigorous. I promise—"

"Don't you dare apologize!" Hera replied emphatically, twisting so she could look him in the eye. "That was the best sex of my life! The only promise you're going to give me is that we can do that again. Do you understand?"

A rumbling purr echoed from Augustine's chest. "You are not just saying that?"

"I don't lie," Hera said quietly. "You should know that by now."

"You passed out."

"From pleasure." Hera wanted to roll her eyes.

"I did not realize that was possible." He blinked slowly at her.

"Believe me, it is, and you just railed me into next week." Hera smirked and squeezed her inner muscles, clamping around his knot and making him groan. "If tonight is what sex with you will be like regularly, I'm going to be a very happy woman."

Augustine hummed and licked her nose, making her laugh. "Your happiness is paramount."

"So... Ummm... When will you deflate?"

# EPILOGUE

AUGUSTINE WOKE UP in the morning in an unfamiliar room on an unfamiliar bed. But the woman with him was easily recognizable. His heart gave a particularly large thump when she rolled onto her back and stretched like a cat, her curvaceous nude body on full display for him.

"Enjoying the view or are you going to participate?" she said, a sleepy rasp in her voice that brought him to instant hardness.

"What would you do if I said I wanted to enjoy the view?" Belying his words, he curled one hand around her hip and stroked his thumb over smooth skin.

She shivered and her skin pebbled under his touch.

Amused, his gaze followed the goosebumps as they covered her body in a wave. "So responsive," he murmured, bringing a fingertip to the swell of her breast, swirling around it in ever-shrinking circles. It heaved, her breathing becoming ragged, and he raised his gaze to her face. "I think I'm addicted to you."

"Good," Hera gasped. "Augustine, please..."

Taking pity on her, he rolled in

between her legs and, using his mouth, brought her pleasure over and over again, her cries music to his ears.

"Hera, I need your hel—" The voice that interrupted his feast came from the door. "Oh my Goddess, I am *so* sorry!"

"No, don't stop, I'm so close!" Hera pressed his head back down, making it clear who she was talking to.

"Seriously?" The voice at the door squeaked.

*Oh Goddess,* Augustine thought, flushing.

"Yes, yes, *yes*!" Hera shouted, her hips thrusting against his face.

He pulled away after she calmed down. "I cannot believe that the first impression your sister has of me is my bare backside while I..."

"Eat me out?" Hera finished dreamily.

"She's the Goddess of fertility and no stranger to the pleasures of the flesh. Besides, your ass is gorgeous."

"I have never heard it referred to as that before," Augustine said dryly, getting to his feet and searching for his clothing.

"Then, you haven't been paying attention," Hera retorted. She clothed herself with a wave of her hand. "I'll go see what Demi wants."

Augustine got dressed quickly and arranged his hair in the mirror before taking a deep breath. "Maybe she's gone," he whispered to himself, opening the door of the bedroom.

She wasn't.

Demi turned to greet him with a smile and slightly flushed cheeks. "Nice to meet you properly," she said, holding out her hand. "Congratulations on your engagement."

"Hera speaks of you often. And thank you."

"All good things, I hope," Demi replied with a chuckle. "There's going to be a barbeque at Lucifer's this afternoon and everyone's invited. He's showing off the baby."

"She's a darling," Hera cooed as she bustled about the kitchen, making breakfast.

"How can I help?" Augustine asked.

"Call your brothers and tell them to come to the barbeque." Hera kissed his cheek and returned to the coffee maker. "Do you prefer dark, medium, or light roast?"

"Uh, coffee?"

"Medium it is," Hera said.

"I'll see you two lovebirds later," Demi said on the way out the door. "Hera, I really do need your help downstairs with the desserts, when you get a chance." She popped her head back in. "Oh, and Augustine, nice ass."

"I am going to die," Augustine muttered under his breath.

"Don't worry, she's not going to tell anyone other than Charles," Hera said.

"That is not reassuring," Augustine replied, dialing the number for his house.

In the end, Hera *and* Augustine, along with Charles, helped get everything ready. Demi was a veritable force of nature in the kitchen, jumping from one project to the next and overseeing her three helpers.

Half an hour before the party, there

was a knock on the back door.

"Friends of yours?" Hera asked Augustine, holding the door open so he could see his brothers' smiling faces.

"Augustine said you might need help," Finley said.

"Perfect timing," Demi said, putting a box in his hands. "The truck is just around the corner."

Augustine smothered a chuckle. "This is Jaden, that was Finley," he said by way of introduction.

The six of them made quick work of packing the truck and headed over to Lucifer and Chloe's.

"They seem nice," Hera whispered to Augustine in the backseat of the truck behind Demi and Charles.

"*Seems* is the operative word," Augustine replied, rolling his eyes. He laughed softly to himself. "But in all seriousness, they're great guys."

Setting up took Demi no longer than a wave of her hand in the large central garden of the castle.

"Thank you," Chloe said, coming up to them. "I know Lucifer sprung this on you rather last minute…"

"It was no problem at all," Demi reassured her. "I had excellent helpers."

Lucifer appeared just then, baby Atlanta snug in his arms, bright eyes looking around in interest. "Ah, there you are, McKellen." His nostrils flared and his eyebrows furrowed. "We haven't seen one of your kind in Purgatory before," he growled.

Augustine swallowed hard, all his nerves on edge and hackles raised. He felt sure that Lucifer was going to order him to leave, that he didn't want dragon shifters in his city…

And then Lucifer laughed, slapping him on the shoulder. "You and your brothers fit right in. We should go flying sometime. Want to hold her?"

"Hold—?" Augustine felt like he'd gotten whiplash.

Lucifer transferred the baby to his arms, giving him no time to think. Augustine looked down at the tiny pink bundle uncertainly. "Good day, little one."

She blinked her eyes slowly, which Augustine decided meant she trusted him.

"You're a natural," Hera said, peeking at the baby over his arm. "We need to help your brothers."

"What do you mean?" He looked

around for them, wondering how they'd gotten in trouble already.

"I mean we should help them find their mates!" Hera exclaimed excitedly. "So they can be as happy as we are!"

"You know, I cannot think of a single reason why not."

Thank you for reading Hera!

If you enjoyed this book, please return to the retailer and leave a review. Your words mean so much and help us to continue writing the books you love.

*Follow our Facebook page here: <u>Speed Dating with the Denizens of the Underworld Series</u>*

*Watch your favorite online retailer for the other books in the Speed Dating with the Denizens of the Underworld series.*

*Turn the page now for an excerpt from Medusa by Gina Kincade, Book Thirty in the Speed Dating with the Denizens of the Underworld series!*

# EXCERPT

MEDUSA, KNOWN AS Maddie to her friends, woke up slowly one grey morning. The gloom outside made her want to curl up under her covers for another couple hours. She stretched languidly and glanced at her alarm clock. It was an old-fashioned kind, with red illuminated numbers.

The numbers were flashing 12:00.

"Shit!" Maddie cursed, grabbing at

her cell phone and almost dropping it in her haste to turn it on. "*Shit!*" she exclaimed again when she saw that it was almost eight in the morning. She whipped her covers off, scrambling gracelessly out of bed and stripping out of her tank top and short shorts that she wore to sleep. She didn't see where they'd landed, because she already had her t-shirt half on. She tucked her bra, underwear, and socks into a bag, yanked on a pair of comfy leggings, and half-ran, half-fell down the stairs.

She looked longingly at her coffee maker, but there was no time for that this morning. She grabbed a banana and granola bar, which joined her garments in the bag, and stepped into her running shoes before she was out the door.

The daycare she owned was only two

blocks away, thankfully, and she sprinted the short distance. She arrived out of breath and disheveled, just as the first parent was walking up the pathway.

"Hestia," she gasped at her assistant. "Do you mind…"

"Not a problem," Hestia reassured her calmly. "Hello Damien, are you excited to play with the dinosaurs again?"

The door closing behind her cut off the rest of the conversation. "First order of business, get properly dressed," Maddie said to herself, closing herself in her office. The clock on the wall told her she'd managed to make it from bed to work in less than five minutes. "Thank someone," she muttered and started fixing her clothing. She practically inhaled her breakfast before rejoining Hestia in the common space.

Damien, age three, was playing with the large plastic dinosaurs they'd received yesterday. There was a Stegosaurus, a Triceratops, and of course, a Tyrannosaurus Rex. Damien had decided that the three-horned dinosaur was the baby and the other two were the parents.

Maddie deftly plucked the screw out of Shana's hands before it reached her mouth, the nine-month-old too young to understand the difference between food and toy. The baby screwed up her face, ready to scream, but then she spotted the dark haired Alexander and made happy babbles at him. The pretty toddler boy was only two, but he already had half the population of Purgatory wrapped around his little finger, and Maddie was no exception. Fortunately, he was a darling and the extra attention didn't do him any harm.

"Maddie," Hestia said in an undertone. "Lady Chloe is here to talk to you."

Maddie's eyebrows rose in surprise. Then she remembered that the Lord of the Underworld's wife worked above, in the human realm, and she'd gone back to her job recently after the birth of their first child six months ago. "I'll talk to her right away. Are you all right with them?" She indicated the kids happily playing on the floor.

"We'll be fine. Shoo," Hestia said gently, waving her hands in the direction of the kitchen. "And have some coffee."

"Yes, Mother," Maddie teased. In reality, she was desperate for the dark shot of caffeine and would probably do almost anything for some. "Hello, Lady Chloe," she greeted the blonde woman in her kitchen.

"Please, drop the honorific," Chloe pleaded. She had baby Atlanta in one arm and a to-go coffee from the ButterNut Bakery in her free hand. "I need to talk to you."

"I'm all ears," Maddie said, pulling down her favorite mug and pouring herself a cup from the coffee maker in the corner.

"Atlanta is..." Chloe trailed off, biting her lip.

Maddie waited patiently, the mug warming her hands as she cradled it.

"You know I'm a wolf shifter, right?" Chloe asked, turning the full force of her gaze on Maddie.

"Yes."

"And Lucifer's a demon."

"Naturally."

"Well… Atlanta's a little precocious." Chloe put the baby down on the ground gently.

The instant the baby's feet touched the tile, she transformed, her back legs becoming like those of a wolf. Tiny, ebony-colored, sparsely feathered wings sprouted from her shoulder blades. The rest of her stayed in human form, and she flopped around her mother's feet, crying piteously.

Chloe picked her up again and Atlanta turned full human once more. Chloe gestured at the baby, shrugging as if to say, "See?"

Maddie grinned. "That was incredible!" She directed her comments to the baby. "You're so good at that!"

"Not so great in a *human* daycare," Chloe said meaningfully. "Please, tell me you have room for her here? I don't know what else to do!"

"Of course we have room for her. I assume you wanted her close to your work so you could pop in and see her during the day," Maddie said.

"Exactly," Chloe interrupted. "But when *this* started happening…"

"I totally understand. Can you stick around this morning, let her get used to Hestia and I before you go during the afternoon?"

"Yes, yes, anything! My boss is fully aware that my hours will be shortened for the next while. They're very understanding, thankfully."

"Why don't we sit and talk?" Maddie suggested to Chloe. To the baby, she asked, "Atlanta, may I carry you to the couch?"

The baby hid her face in her mother's shoulder and Maddie nodded. "That's just fine. I'm a complete stranger to you."

Chloe chuckled. "Actually, she might be a little startled by your hair."

"My hair?" Maddie repeated, startled. "What..." She caught a glimpse of herself in the reflection cast by the window. "Yikes, that's quite the bedhead!" She immediately started running her fingers through the brilliant crimson strands, trying to calm it down. "There must have been a power surge or outage at my place last night. My alarm didn't go off this morning. I made it here with only seconds to spare!"

"Impressive," Chloe said.

After her hair was somewhat tamed, Maddie led the way to one of the squashy couches, grabbing a couple different sensory toys on the way, to help the baby get to know her.

She alternated conversations between mother and child. "You like the zebra?" Maddie asked the fascinated infant, who was now sitting comfortably on her mother's lap. "Would you like to hold it?"

The baby didn't make any movement to grab it, so Maddie made it prance across the distance between them and up Chloe's thigh. At the top, the zebra seemed to see the girl and shied away from her, hiding on the couch cushion.

"This is Atlanta. She's new here. It's okay to be a little scared of new things, Mister Zebra." Maddie deepened her voice to speak for the zebra, "I don't like new things! I only like you!" Back to her normal voice, she continued the one-sided conversation, "Aww, that's sweet. But I know you'll absolutely love Atlanta once you get to know her."

Atlanta leaned so far forward to see the stuffed animal that Chloe had to catch her before she fell off her mother's lap. "Ba!" the baby said, making grabby hands. "Bababa!"

"Zebra," Maddie enunciated clearly. "You would like the zebra?"

"Ba!" she shrieked delightedly when the zebra's head popped into her sight again, her wings reappearing on her back. She grabbed for the animal and Maddie surrendered the toy gracefully.

"I assume you would like to encourage her shifting?" Maddie said to Chloe while Atlanta was distracted with turning the animal around in her hands.

"Yes, of course." Chloe leaned back against the cushions and took a sip of her coffee. "Her wings are too fragile to carry her weight, as slight as she is, so we'll need to build up her muscles."

"As with any other muscle group at this age," Maddie agreed. "May I touch the wings?" she asked both of them.

Chloe nodded and Atlanta ignored her, so Maddie gently ran a finger over the top edge. "Similar to a baby bird with how the bones are arranged, soft down feathers, those will fluff out in time," Maddie muttered under her breath.

"You just had to mention the lack of feathers," Chloe put in, amused.

Maddie blushed. "Sorry. I assume they're similar to her father's?"

"Lucifer's are much bigger, but they

do seem to be built along the same lines," Chloe replied.

"How do you feel about her exploring on her own in the house and in the yard?" Maddie asked. "We can, of course, wear her if you'd prefer she not be let down..." she trailed off, letting Chloe talk.

"She does love to be held," Chloe said thoughtfully. "But I think letting her figure things out on her own would be good for her. It might encourage her to transform into a wolf the full way. You're fully fenced in, right?"

"Yes, and we keep a close eye on them at all times in case something dangerous made its way into the grounds and we missed it. What does she eat?"

"I'll give you a couple of bottles of

breastmilk every day, one for mid-morning, one for mid-afternoon. At lunch, she can have whatever the others are having, in bite-sized portions. She especially likes to feed herself cheese." Chloe smiled.

"Dairy isn't a problem, then?"

"No, no dietary restrictions that we've found so far. We've tested all the usual human and wolf intolerances, just to be safe."

"Smart," Maddie said. "Two naps?"

"Yes, one hour at ten and two hours at one-thirty, although if you wear her or she's feeling under the weather, she'll sleep longer."

"Naturally. Would you like to see the nap setup?" At Chloe's nod, Maddie reached out to Atlanta again. "May I hold you?"

The baby launched herself gleefully into her arms, making Maddie laugh and smile down at the child. "I like you, too."

She led Chloe to a room beyond the kitchen that had several portable cribs set up. "We can move them around, depending on the child. Some prefer to sleep in a noisy environment, so we would bring the crib into the main room for them. On hot days, we pull them outside and set up sun shades in the breezeway."

"That's fantastic," Chloe said enthusiastically. "Should we bring anything from home for her?"

"Anything you think might make her feel more comfortable. For children as young as Atlanta, we generally suggest a t-shirt that you've worn recently, so that they can smell something comforting that reminds them of home. Breastmilk, of course. Diapers, if she has sensitive skin. We don't put any diaper cream, unless she's having troubles, because it's better for their skin to breathe. When were you thinking of potty training her?" Maddie kept her expression neutral.

Chloe laughed. "We haven't even considered potty training yet! When she shows interest in it, I guess."

"That's a good attitude to have. Every child reacts differently to potty training, and you don't want to push her into something before she's ready for it. We will follow your lead on potty training when it's time, so that she doesn't get mixed messages." Maddie led them back into the playroom.

Atlanta froze when she saw the other children, the zebra dangling by one leg from her mouth.

Maddie chuckled. "Would you like to play with them?" She sat cross-legged on the ground and put Atlanta in the relative safety of her lap. "This is Shana, Alexander, and Damien." She pointed at each child in turn, who mostly didn't look up from what they were doing.

Encouraged by their disinterest in a new playmate, Atlanta reached out for a nearby block and swapped the zebra for it, drool running down her chin.

"Teething, are you?" Maddie said. "We'll get you a frozen teether and put it with Lyta's. She can commiserate with you, poor thing."

"Her fifth," Chloe supplied, sitting beside them.

"And you're still nursing her? Brave woman," Maddie said.

Chloe laughed ruefully. "She learned *very* quickly not to bite me or she'd lose access to her food."

"That would do it," Maddie said, smiling in sympathy.

"I'm so glad you had space for her," Chloe said, reaching out and squeezing Maddie's hand. "Human-wolf babies with wings are rather frowned upon in Earth daycares."

Maddie almost choked on her laughter. "You think?"

Snag your copy of Medusa at your favorite online retailer.

Watch for the other books in the
Speed Dating with the Denizens of the
Underworld Series

Lucifer

Samael

Hecate

Demi

Hell's Belle

Hades

Orion

Cassiel

Hera

Triton

Alastor

Athena

Zeus

Medusa

Spike

Artemis

Calliope

# HERA

Mars

Pegasus

And More!

# MORE FROM GINA

If you enjoyed this book, you may also enjoy…

**Blackthorn Academy**

Witch's Delight

Witch's Mystery

Witch's Pet

Witch's Baby

**Speed Dating with the Denizens of the Underworld**

Lucifer

Demi

Hera

Medusa

Artemis

# FOLLOW GINA

Facebook
https://www.facebook.com/authorginakincade/

Newsletter Mailing List
https://landing.mailerlite.com/webforms/landing/r1r5n4

BookBub
https://www.bookbub.com/authors/gina-kincade

Blog/Webpage:
https://www.ginakincade.com/

Instagram
https://www.instagram.com/ginakincade/

Goodreads
https://www.goodreads.com/ginakincade

# ABOUT GINA KINCADE

USA Today Bestselling Author Gina Kincade spends her days tapping away at a keyboard, through blood, sweat, and often many tears, crafting steamy paranormal romances filled with shifters and vampires, along with witchy urban fantasy tales in magical worlds she hopes her readers yearn to crawl into.

A busy mom of three, she loves healthy home cooking, gardening, warm beaches, fast cars, and horseback riding.

Ms. Kincade's life is full, time is never on her side, and she wouldn't change a moment of it!

Find more from Gina at:
https://www.ginakincade.com/

www.ingramcontent.com/pod-product-compliance
Lightning Source LLC
Chambersburg PA
CBHW061056210726
48294CB00001B/168